TRISTESSA & LUCIDO

Photo credit: Bruce Hart

Miriam Zolin grew up in Melbourne and East Gippsland in Victoria and currently lives in Sydney.

Before, during and after studying linguistics, languages and literature at the University of New England in Armidale (in northern NSW), Miriam has had a varied working life, doing everything from marking lambs and washing dishes, through to nannying, managing a corporate intranet and running the offices of at least two pseudo-government organisations. More recently, she has been developing a career as a technical writer and process analyst, creating user manuals and other documentation for business, computer software, networks and hardware. She keeps herself amused by scaring her managers in the corporate world with her insistence that some of her greatest works of fiction have the words *User Manual* on the front cover.

Miriam's first novel *Most Beloved* was short-listed for the Australian Vogel Literary Award in 1992. She has had a number of articles published in magazines with subjects as varied as self-sufficiency lifestyles and jazz. Her short story 'Between Come and Go' was published in the 2001 University of Technology, Sydney (UTS) Writers Anthology *Small Suburban Crimes*.

Visit Miriam's website at www.miriamzolin.com

TRISTESSA & LUCIDO

a novel by

MIRIAM ZOLIN

for Lesley Helen

First published 2003 by University of Queensland Press
Box 6042, St Lucia, Queensland 4067 Australia

www.uqp.uq.edu.au

© Miriam Zolin

Typeset by University of Queensland Press
Printed in Australia by McPherson's Printing Group

Distributed in the USA and Canada by
International Specialized Book Services, Inc.,
5824 N.E. Hassalo Street, Portland, Oregon 97213–3640

Cataloguing in Publication Data
National Library of Australia

Zolin, Miriam, 1964– .
  Tristessa and Lucido.

  I. Title.

A823.4

ISBN 0 7022 3372 2

PROLOGUE

You remember the day you were born. The feeling of separation, and the wash of human sorrow through your body, the way your fingertips and toes felt as you became your own self, separating from the whole like a bubble of oil in a warm lava lamp. You remember the electricity of selfness that arced just once but unmistakably between your tiny fingers and the great comfort you received from the arms that quickly enfolded you and the breast you suckled soon afterwards; the milk that went some small and strangely unsatisfying way towards feeding this hungry thing that you were.

You remember a shaft of sunlight through the window high above your crib, specks of something dancing in the stream of afternoon light, and your hand reaching to touch them and instead sending them swirling even faster in the gold. You remember lying on your back communing with all the things that you could see. There was no thing you could not talk to and you talked to every thing.

You remember crawling. Crawling seemed a fine thing to be doing, until you answered some unspoken need to stand upright on your strong little legs. With wits and tiny clenched fists you pulled yourself up to the edge of the glass coffee table and suddenly the world was filled with things you absolutely had to have though you had not even known they existed just a few minutes before.

And so the search began, fed by a hunger that you never named because it was never separate from who you were. The concept of *I* or *me* came with a need that was simply in you. And you spent a part of every day feeding it or planning how to.

PROSPECT

While she powders her nose in the restroom at Jo Jo's Grill, you survey the bar. The two of you have been here since half-past ten this evening and it's definitely time to go. The crowd here is getting rowdy with alcohol. The music is crap and your head is beginning to thump in time to the beat. The Princess isn't going to find a new boyfriend here, and the last thing you need is for her to get bored and restless. You have watched her like a mother hen all evening, thinking you are more aware than she is of the sparrowhawks that circle her, the foxes and the wild dogs that slaver at the thought of her juicy bones. On nights like this, you count her drinks, and gauge her drunkenness and remind her to slow down or to have a glass of water when you see she might be nearing some sort of danger zone.

She returns and as she sits down, a young man approaches.

'What are you drinking?' he asks her.

Before she can answer, you say 'We're just leaving, actually.'

He looks at you, then at her. She shrugs. You rise out

of your chair. She picks up her purse and starts to rummage around in it for a cigarette. You sit down again.

'You could stay for one more drink,' he says. 'Come sit with me and my friends.' He points over to where they are sitting.

You both look over to the group he indicates and after a moment's assessment the Princess looks at you, one eyebrow raised. There is a moment's pause and then, simultaneously, the two of you give each other a tiny shake of the head, and burst out giggling. Not surprisingly, he goes back to his friends.

You help the Princess on with her coat and guide her out the door and to the car. She sways provocatively in that way she has that draws the eyes of every man in every bar. The swaying has an effect on you too. It makes you feel faint embarrassment, and disgust at the openly lustful stares that she attracts. None of the leering is for you. Sometimes you are hypersensitive to all the differences between you — the things that make her desirable to all who see her and the things you have that can be discovered only with a little time and effort.

Outside, a cold Nebraska wind is blowing. The wind that gives new meaning to the term wind chill factor. And yet tonight is not so bad. There's snow coming so the air is relatively warm. On the coldest windy days here in the wintry Mid-West of America, the weather channel reminds viewers to ensure that exposed flesh is covered in winds like this.

With arms linked, the two of you walk quickly over to your car, taking care not to slip on the ice as you go. As you drive out of the parking lot, she lights the cigarette she finally found in the packet at the bottom of her purse. When she speaks, she sounds surprisingly sober.

'Thanks for looking after me,' she says. And then 'Are you okay with this?' looking at you clearly.

You turn to her and smile. 'Sure I am. That's what friends are for, isn't it?'

This simple lie is a snapshot of your entire friendship. Later tonight, or maybe tomorrow morning, depending how long this night goes on, you will be crying on your sofa or in your bed, crying from loneliness or something for which loneliness is as good a name as any. Nights like this with her always seem to make it worse. You have tried to work out why this should be so, but no satisfactory answer has ever presented itself. It is just the way it is.

DOTTIE'S NOTEBOOK

Dottie asked me to write this and somehow I never started until now; but now that she has gone, and I have ended up in Prospect, Nebraska, I realise I have to do it. Dottie said I didn't understand my past. She said we're all on a journey and she said that the only way to live successfully is to really be in the present. The only way to be in the present, she said, is to have understood and moved on from the past.

I can feel my past beginning to surface again, and I don't want it to ruin my present. I don't want to believe that it is inevitable. And since the part of the past that haunts me is all about this thing I can do — this alleged gift — then I've decided to concentrate on that. If I can understand that part of me, perhaps the rest of it will begin to make sense. Perhaps I will stop wanting to run away.

My name is Athena Frances Fairweather and I have a gift. The first time I remember using it I was six and we were in the middle of a drought.

Dad said it was the worst year yet. Every day we found

more ewes dead out in the paddocks — dead from starvation and exhaustion. My father took the sheep out to what we called the long paddock, sometimes for a week at a time, allowing them to graze along the edges of the quiet roads around the property. But eventually even this grass disappeared and the cloudless skies pressed down on the farm. On and on it went, month after month. Nobody had seen anything like it. Tanker trucks brought water in so that we could at least keep some stock alive. Dad stored a portion of the oat harvest each year in silos he had built especially in the paddock next to the woolshed. He used the grain during the drought to feed the sheep. He taught me how to drive the tractor that year, blocking up the pedals so my legs could reach, showing me how to steer in a wide circle over the cracked, dry paddocks, while he stood on the carry-all at the back and held a grain bag out, trickling oats out in a line on the ground. He said the ewes had to be kept in good enough condition that they would conceive when we put the ram over them.

It was a year that smelled of oat dust, earth dust, sheep urine and diesel fumes. Then lambing came and the drought still hadn't broken. Exhausted, malnourished ewes struggled to give birth so we had to help them. Dad took me with him to the lambing paddock in the pre-dawn. He said that lambs like to be born in the early morning, sometimes before the sun has given any light to the sky.

The first cold dark June morning that he took me to the lambs I heard their little cries and I also felt — sensed somehow — the confusion and fear of their mothers. I had no idea that Dad couldn't feel their pain the same way I could. I thought everyone was like me.

In the dark unmoonlit inkness of the lambing paddock, I walked behind my father and learned from him, watching what he did.

'Here, Theney,' he said, 'Come here.'

He squatted beside a ewe who was in terrible distress. She struggled to get to her feet, and I could see four little lamb legs protruding from her vulva.

'Hold her down, Theney,' he said. 'I have to help her. The lamb's turned and she can't push it out on her own.'

I felt how much she wanted to get away. She was in agony, and terrified. Sheep have different lights around them than people, but you wouldn't even have to see the light to see how she felt.

'Put your knee on her shoulder near her neck, gently, like this,' and he showed me what to do to keep her still. 'Don't choke her … she's frightened. But if you rest your knee here, she won't be able to get up.'

But when he moved away, I didn't do what he had said. Instead, I kneeled beside her head, and put my hand on her neck, then touched her on the forehead, between her eyes. I looked into her eye. 'There, there,' I said, and she stopped struggling and lay quiet.

'Theney! I told you to put your knee …' Dad's voice trailed off. 'How did you do that?'

I was surprised he didn't know. 'I just took it away.'

'Took it …?'

'That thing on top, the scared thing. I took it away.'

He looked at me for a long minute and I wondered if I'd done something wrong.

'Keep her still,' he finally said. 'This will make her buck.'

And he pushed the lamb back inside her, twisted it around and helped her give birth. When he pulled the lamb out it fell to the ground in an ungainly heap, and he quickly cleaned its mouth and nose passages.

'Let her up, Theney, and come stand by me,' he said. 'Come see a miracle.'

He stepped back and I went and stood beside him. The ewe stood up and turned to sniff her lamb. She licked the slimy sac that covered it and it made a little bleating noise, raising its too-big head.

'See,' said Dad gently, his big calloused hand tightening around my little soft one. 'See, they know each other.'

I smiled up at him. I so loved my father when I saw him like this. And then I felt a stab of something sharp in my heart, and pulled my hand out of his.

'What?' he said. 'What's the matter, Theney?'

I listened carefully, though it was not my ears that listened. It was some other part of me. I found the source and pointed, not saying a word. In the grey early morning, we could see a ewe running, terrified, away from the flock and right behind her was a fox. He was snapping at her, and I could see something sticking out.

'Oh, no,' said Dad. He knelt down so he was my height and looked into my eyes with a serious expression on his face. He put his hand on my shoulder. 'Stay here Theney. Stay right here.'

He ran towards the sheep. She was tired, and in the

middle of giving birth, so he caught her easily. The fox stopped, hesitated, then ran off, turning every few paces to look back.

I ran over. The need to be there was bigger than any impulse to do what I was told. 'Dad! Daddy! The lamb's hurting.'

'Theney, I told you to stay over there. You should have stayed there, where I told you.'

'Daddy, the lamb …'

'I know. Since you're here, hold the ewe down, but don't look. All right? Just don't look.'

I couldn't help looking. I could feel its pain. I had to see. It was that simple — I had to see.

But what I saw was so horrible it made me cry out. 'Daddy, its mouth!'

The starving fox, itself a victim of the drought, had bitten off the lamb's lips and tongue, even before it was born. The face of that poor little thing was a bloody mess. I looked at my father and I could feel what it did to him, the black sorrow that welled up, the anger …

'We have to kill it Theney, it's the only way. We have to kill it. Don't watch.'

'Daddy, let me hold it.'

His voice was sharp. 'No Theney. No nonsense. I'm going to cut its throat. There's no other way.'

'I know Daddy. I know.' Tears poured down my face. 'But let me hold it.' I reached my arms out. But he wouldn't let me hold it, even though all I wanted was to take that brand new little creature's fear away, and help it die in peace. Something in me shifted at the awful cruelty. Why wouldn't he let me help?

10

As he cut its throat, I felt its fear like a sharp thing in my own stomach. 'Noooo!' and I was sobbing inconsolably. He had to pick me up and carry me back to the truck.

He drove me home in silence, and then went out there again, on his own.

I heard him talking to Mum later. 'You should have seen it Christine,' he said. 'She sort of touched it here.' A pause. 'You should have seen her crying when I wouldn't let her hold the lamb.'

'Perhaps she got it, John. Perhaps it skipped to her.'

'Nonsense,' he said. 'There's never been any sign. She's normal. Probably just needs to get used to it. Farm life's hard, she'll toughen up.'

PROSPECT

If you count Jo Jo's, and Paddy McGuire's, and the seedy bar on Maple whose name you can never remember, then you have already been to three bars before you walk in the door of Linklatters. You have been to three bars and it is nearly midnight and you are still sober.

Linklatters is a place you like to hang out. On Sunday afternoons they have a live jazz trio that plays standards and attracts a crowd you like to watch. It's a place you generally come to on your own, but for a change this evening you do not walk into Linklatters alone. This evening you are escorting the Princess.

While you hold open the door for her to pass through, you stamp the snow off your shoes. You wore high heels tonight, after nearly half an hour of agonised decision-making. As you deposit the last compacted ice on the Linklatters' doormat, you smile to yourself. When you are out with the Princess you could wear a paper bag and bare feet and no one would notice. The Princess takes over a room just by being in it. It does not do to start an evening with the Princess with even the tiniest hint of loneliness in your heart. An evening with her can break a lonely woman into a million little pieces.

She walks into Linklatters and you watch the effect she has on the room and the effect it has on her. Making an entrance is one of her favourite things and she never tires of it. You close the door and follow her. She will choose a place to sit and you will sit beside her and a new chapter in the evening will begin. She chooses a seat at the bar, with a view of the door. You would have preferred a table.

Lloyd is behind the bar tonight. He asks if you'll have the usual and you tell him yes. The usual used to be a gin and tonic, and more specifically Tanqueray. Despite the fact that you always used to think it was pure and simple just a wank to specify the gin you want with your mixer, Tanqueray *does* taste different and at one stage in not-too-distant history your tongue had accustomed itself to it so that when you ordered gin and tonic and started to drink you could tell, Heaven help you, when it wasn't Tanqueray. It was a brief foray into regular non-sobriety and it scared you more than almost anything to realise that you could not get through a day without the taste of juniper berries at the back of your throat.

More recently, your usual has become Shiraz since, homesick and winterised, you long for the sun that made those Australian varietals so peppery and raspberry. You drink Shiraz more slowly and you rarely have more than two in an evening. Lloyd has kept track of your transition from Tanqueray and tonic to Shiraz, and he remembers that you always have a tall glass of water with your drink.

He takes the Princess' order while he pours your wine. The Princess takes a cigarette out of her tiny purse and holds it in one hand, with her wrist extended and exposed and her head thrown slightly back. Looking at her, you know that if you were a man you would see her neck and throat and that is almost all you would see because for a man looking at that sort of woman, who carries herself as though she knows she is beautiful, then nothing else really does matter except the neck and the throat and the way the woman holds them out to you. Lloyd lights her cigarette and asks her if she wants three olives or four in her vodka martini.

The Princess can flirt with anyone, at any time. 'Why Lloyd!' she says. 'What do you think, Honey? I'll take whatever you can give me.'

Sometimes you despair for her. With a well-practised flick of the wrist, Lloyd slides a napkin onto the bar and places the Princess' drink onto it, perfectly centred. He's an artist.

'And what brings you two lovely ladies out into the snowy night?' he asks.

The Princess will answer, and you wonder what she will say. She has decided to be dramatic — you can tell by the way she is positioning herself on the seat, leaning forward just a little. A man, two seats down the bar, is looking at her arse as she sticks it out provocatively. You glower at him and he looks away.

'My heart is broken,' says the Princess. 'We're out tonight to find someone to mend my broken heart.'

Lloyd is all bartender sympathy. 'And how is it going?' he asks.

The Princess pouts and toys with her glass.

'We've been sifting through some weirdos,' you say.

'Well good luck,' says Lloyd and moves down the bar to freshen someone else's drink.

You turn to say something to the Princess, but she has engaged in conversation with the man who was two seats away. He has moved next to her and is obviously entranced, and has ideas. The Princess seems to have the upper hand. She is toying with him, offering up the inside of her perfectly tanned wrist. Her cigarette has gone out and as he re-lights it he tries to see down her blouse and up her skirt at the same time.

Lloyd returns to where you sit at the bar and smiles at you. 'Is she behaving herself tonight?'

You grin at him. 'Does she ever?' He laughs.

The Princess hears you and looks across in mock upset. 'Theney, you are so mean to me!'

The man at the bar touches her shoulder, bends his head to her ear and quietly says something to her that makes her laugh, tinkling, with her head thrown back. He grins at her and walks unsteadily in the direction of the restrooms, down the stairs at the back. Without really knowing why, you motion the Princess to the end seat in the row and you sidle on to the seat beside her. Now there is no seat available for him when he returns.

He lurches back up the stairs and walks towards the two of you and when he reaches the bar, looks around, hesitates, then props himself against the edge and looks bemused. He knows there was a barstool there before.

'Hey mate,' you say and he looks across at you. He registers the double surprise of Australian accent and the imperative tone in a female voice. You are almost as surprised yourself. This is coming from somewhere you haven't been for a very long time. 'Hey mate,' you say again, patting the stool beside you, 'There's a seat here.'

He lurches over and sits down and says he loves your accent. You look at Lloyd and Lloyd (bless him) is rolling his eyes and suppressing a smile as he polishes wine glasses. Lloyd knows what you think about people who love your accent.

'I love you British people,' says the drunk, 'with your Queen and your cute accents.' He sees your glass is empty. 'Lemme getcha drink. What do Brits drink anyways? Ha! Ha! Ha!'

The Princess slides off her stool and says in her best Southern accent, the one that makes them fall at her feet, 'She is Austraaalian, not British,' and teeters across the floorboards in the direction of the restrooms.

'Hey barkeep!' says drunken-bum-know-nothing beside you, trying to attract Lloyd's attention, 'Two more drinks for the ladies'. To you he puts his hand out and says, 'My name is Les. Your friend is real cute'. He says Les with the soft "ess" sound that makes it sound like "less". That cracks you up.

'Yeah,' you say. 'She's engaged to that Huskers quarterback.'

'You kiddin'?' Les is incredulous. Even from this distance, you are acutely aware of the emptiness that he has tried to drown with too many beers. You feel sorry for him but you know you must keep him away from the Princess.

'Yeah,' you say. 'I'm kidding.' It's been so long since

you felt this, and you try, unsuccessfully to stop it. It flows through you and you know you are about to say or do things that you shouldn't. You try and hold back at least, minimise the damage. And then, before you know it, you are leaning towards him. You put your hand on his shoulder and smile into his eyes, which widen in surprise as he feels something in your touch.

Lloyd arrives on cue. 'This gentleman bothering you, Theney?'

'No, thank you, Lloyd,' you say, letting go. 'Not any more. But thanks so much for caring.'

Les wanders off looking back at you over his shoulder, almost fearfully, and Lloyd cocks an eyebrow at you, shakes his head and makes a clucking noise of disapproval.

You suddenly just want to go home. Something about what just happened makes you want to lie in your dark bed and breathe deeply to calm yourself. Is this what Dottie meant when she said it comes back sometimes to bite you on the bum? Where had that urge to touch him come from? Who was the Theney that could touch a total stranger and make him walk away in fear? You down a third of your fresh glass of Shiraz in one gulp and then hold the glass by the stem, swirling the dark liquid so it catches the light and distracts you.

When the Princess returns she sees you want to go. No extrasensory perception required. 'Just this drink,' she says. 'And then we'll go.'

DOTTIE'S NOTEBOOK

There wasn't anything about that Friday afternoon to warn me it was going to be different. As he got out of the car outside the Tattersalls Hotel Dad said the same thing he always did when it was just the two of us. 'We'll just stop here for a bit.' He came around to my side of the car, like he always did, and opened the door.

'Hop out, Theney,' he said, smiling at me as I unbuckled myself and climbed down from the cabin. 'You run in and tell Mrs O'Brien what you want for lunch, and remember,' he said, hand on my shoulder, pretending to be stern, 'don't you go bothering her with your chatter and don't you talk to any strangers. There's a good girl.'

'Okay Dad,' I said and quickly put my arms around his neck and gave him a kiss on the cheek, smelling his Dad smell for a minute before he pushed me away playfully and said 'Go on with you, missy!' But smiling, nevertheless. I watched him go into the main door of the pub and then went round the side, to the lounge.

This was our routine every time he took me in to town to collect the mail or get supplies. Unless Mum was with us, of course. If Mum was there we all went to the Parthenon Café in Main Street where the only dues paid to the Hellenic ancestry of Con and Agape who owned the place were the mousaka *(sic)*, tzatziki and taramosalata (with toast) on the menu that was otherwise filled with such delicacies as veal schnitzel, Hawaiian pizza (with ham and pineapple), chicken Maryland, chicken in a basket, T-bone steak and fisherman's basket.

Mum always had the sole. Whole grilled lemon sole. Dad always had the T-bone and salad. I always had chicken in a basket. A little cane basket with alternating strands of white and gold painted cane so it seemed to be made of something precious. Con used to give me a chocolate milkshake if I wanted it. He would pat me on the head with his big happy hand and tell me that I was a princess. I liked Con.

But sometimes, like on this day, Mum stayed at home and Dad took me in to town on his own. He let me go to the lounge bar and drink lemonade while he downed a few pots in the front bar and talked to other farmers about crops and tractors and the drought. Mrs O'Brien, the publican's wife, made me some lunch and I would read whatever book I was currently stuck on, read it quietly in the cool dark sweet beer and lingering cigarette smoke wood panelling of the lounge bar where, Mrs O'Brien said, ladies used to have to drink, when they weren't allowed into the front bar, before the laws changed. I don't remember seeing anybody ever drinking in there.

On this day, I read my book, and drank my lemonade, didn't bother Mrs O'Brien, just like I'd been told. I remember it was the first book of the Narnia series by C.S.

Lewis. *The Lion, the Witch and the Wardrobe,* the story of those four children who found a secret world through the back of a wardrobe. Books were like secret worlds anyway, where anything was possible, and if those four children could find a world in the back of an old wardrobe, it was easier to understand why I could see people's sadness, and take it away from them with my hands. I had only just begun to realise that what I did was different, and something nobody else could do.

This particular afternoon, a man came into the lounge. An old man, in a grey suit. In fact, everything about him seemed grey. He smelled of stale cigarettes. I smelled them almost before he stepped into the room. He came towards me, smiled and held up a bag of lollies. Licorice allsorts, all different colours, that he'd bought from the front bar where they were raising money for the Spastic Society.

'Hello, little miss,' he said, smiling and showing the gaps. I smiled back. I knew I shouldn't, I knew Dad would be angry if he knew, but I also knew there was nothing harmful about this man. I could see his loneliness oozing from him, into the lolly bag, almost dripping from the frayed ends of his sleeves. The light that surrounded him was uneasy, patchy from the salt of unwept tears or of tears wept privately into a dusty mattress covered with stained ticking in a boarding house he once could never have imagined living in. Something in him was tight and hard and something else in him was dying as a direct consequence. He caught in my throat as he walked across the room towards me. I couldn't say anything, and I couldn't tear my eyes away, although I knew that it was rude to stare like this.

'Hello little miss,' he said. 'I knew your grandfather. We used to play billiards after the war.'

'Hello,' I said. 'But I'm not supposed to talk to you. My father said I shouldn't. I mean … I shouldn't talk to anyone,' I paused. 'He said.' I could feel his ache, and my own heartstrings pulled tight in response.

And then, somehow, I heard myself speak a thought out loud. 'I'm sorry you're sad,' I said. I clapped my hand to my mouth. Where had that come from? I could almost hear my mother's voice *'Where are your manners, Theney?'*

'Ah,' he said with a short laugh. 'You're Dot's grand-daughter, all right. Would you like a lolly?' He sat down at the table across from me and pulled the top of the packet open. 'You know, that's exactly what she said to me last time I saw her,' he said. '"I'm sorry that you're so sad, Tom" — musta been thirty-five years ago, before your mother was born. Just out of the blue like that, like you just said it. She's always been a bit different.' He smiled at me. 'I nearly married your grandmother,' he said. 'I suppose that means I could have been your grand-father, doesn't it?' He handed the opened packet of licorice allsorts across the table. 'Take one,' he said. 'Your dad won't mind.'

As I reached out to take a lolly from the bag my hand touched his, and I felt it then, the terrible, terrible emp-tiness that caused him more suffering than I had ever imagined could exist. And just after I stiffened with the fear of what such pain could do to me if I let it in, I felt a clear knowledge, a pure understanding of what I could do for him. An absence of choice. An overwhelming impulse. I pulled my twelve-year-old hand off his gnarly life-bitten one, walked around the table and placed my right hand on his heart. I felt the pain begin to clear away, to dislodge; felt the tightness in him relax and saw the light around him clear a little.

He looked at me with his watery old eyes brimming over. The corners of his mouth turned down and a moan came out of him. I felt him start to let go of the thing inside he held so tight.

Suddenly, my father's voice rang out behind me, making me jump. '*What!*'

I hadn't heard footsteps, hadn't heard him coming, and now he stood in the doorway, looking somehow three metres tall. I pulled my hand away from the old man's chest and backed away from him, a step, two steps.

'What the fuck's going on here?' yelled Dad.

The old man looked up at him, helpless, his eyes wet from what I had just done. 'Sorry mate, sorry John … John, you know me … I meant nothing. Sorry little miss.'

And then Dad lifted the man bodily from his chair with his left hand around his shirt collar and took a swing with his right hand. His fist connected with the old face, and the grey body slumped then fell to the floor of the lounge bar, ending up lying sprawled on the swirling carpet.

Mrs O'Brien came running in then, 'John! John Fairweather, you leave him alone.' She fell to her knees beside the grey man on the carpet and lifted his head.

'What were you thinking? He's an old man. Oh my God, he's unconscious.'

A crowd had started filling the lounge bar, and Mrs O'Brien looked up from where she knelt on the floor.

'Get him out of here,' she said to her husband, indicating Dad with her head. 'He's drunk.'

He wasn't though, he wasn't drunk. I could tell. But he was angry and frightened. I felt the fear zapping around him. And he was frightened of me. Of me. I felt the tears sitting, waiting, but I managed not to cry them.

'Don't touch me,' he yelled to all the people milling around. 'I'm leaving. Fucking pervert.' And to me, '*You*, come with me,' and he grabbed my shoulder and wrenched me out the door to the car.

'Put your seatbelt on,' he said, 'and if I ever catch you …' He left the rest unsaid, but I knew enough. It was all my fault.

I spent the drive home in a fog. A tiredness had somehow got into my bones. 'Don't talk to me,' he said. 'Don't say a fucking word. I know about this thing you've got and you'd better pray it goes away, because I'm not having any of it.'

PROSPECT

Suddenly, in the hum and bustle of Linklatters on a Saturday night, there is Aubrey, though you don't know his name yet. You suppose he knows the Princess because he walks towards the two of you with purpose. The first thing you notice about him is the way the light attaches itself to his ragged edges. It takes you by surprise to see the light of him, to see him shining in this place. The last time you saw light like this around a person … But no, you cannot think of that here. You must not remember that now, because it always catches you up in sadness and you need to be alone to let that happen. You had managed to reduce the amount of time you spent thinking about it. You could almost go a day without a single glancing memory of Daniel and his light. And now here, in Linklatters, with its subdued low-wattage globes and dark wood and green marble, there is a stranger posing some sort of question suddenly with his own surprising silver-liquid light. A light that no one else can see.

The second thing you notice about Aubrey Meadows, somewhere between the light and his dinner suit, incongruous with no other dinner suits in sight, is that he is looking at you. Straight at you. He glances at the Princess, of course. The glance at her is obligatory, but you realise that it represents the bare minimum of deference required in her presence. Before and after the glance in her direction he looks only at you.

You register his light but you make a point of barely glancing at him. The smile you bestow in response to his 'Hi' is polite, fleeting. He holds out his hand and you find yourself putting your own in his and leaving it there.

He tightens his fingers gently around yours. 'Aubrey,' he says, and holds on for just a breath more than he should.

Something stirs. Awkwardly you pull your hand away and speak directly to the Princess, turning the side of your face to this raggedy intruder.

'It's my turn to visit the bathroom,' you say.

The barstool scrapes as you stand. The doorway to the basement, where the restrooms are, seems to get further away as you try to move towards it. When you reach the top of the stairs and look down them you see how steep and dangerous they are and you hold onto the handrail all the way down. You know you must hold on. You know that if you let go you will fall and break something.

In the mirror downstairs you look into your own eyes and try to think of something, but nothing comes. Something stirs, but it is not thought. It is not anything you can stop or start. You wish there were a back door you could use to run away.

DOTTIE'S NOTEBOOK

The only one who understood was my aunt Dottie. She and Dad never really got on, but she always made the effort to spend time with me. She used to come and help out on the farm at shearing time, at lambing time, at hay-making … and the year that I turned fourteen was the year that my mother first got sick and Dottie came to help.

Dottie knew. Dottie knew it all. She knew when she saw me holding Granny Dot's hand at the hospice in town. I went there every week with Mum but this week Dottie took me because Mum was feeling tired. In the car on the way home, she asked me questions and nodded when I answered them — as though she had known all along that I could do this thing I did, see the things I saw.

'Theney, sweetheart,' she said. 'You have a gift. Let me tell you about your Granny Dot. Something special about her that hardly anyone knows.'

Granny Dot, who never spoke and had to be fed with a spoon.

'Your grandmother was a healer,' said Dottie. And

'Your grandmother could see auras. She could do these things until she had her first child — your mother. That's how it's passed. Sometimes it skips a generation. Sometimes it moves sideways. So I got a little bit of it, and your mother never had it. But she passed it on to you. Does she know?'

I shook my head. 'I asked once … but it was too hard. She wouldn't talk about it. I think Dad knows, but it scares him. It makes him angry.'

Dottie looked at me for a long moment, then kissed my forehead. 'Blessings on your little head, my love,' she said. 'You have a good heart.' She was quiet for a moment. 'Theney, I'm going to start spending more time in America. You know I go there sometimes?'

I just looked at her.

'I love it in San Antonio,' she said. 'It's my home now — one of them.' She smiled. 'I'd like you to come and see me in my house there one summer, if your parents will let you. I'll ask them before I go. It's a beautiful place, Texas. I think you'd love it. I can take you for a drive to the Hill Country. When it's the time of year for Blue Bonnets, the hills are covered with carpets of them.' She looked wistfully into the middle distance, then reached across and touched me on the knee. 'But no matter what, Theney, you'll always have me. You can come to me any time, or call me if you need me. I'm here for you.'

Later that night, when I was supposed to be in bed, I stood in the passageway outside the kitchen, listening as my father shouted at her 'Get out of my house, Doris.' He always called her Doris.

My mother murmured something to placate him but it seemed to have the opposite effect and he shouted even louder, at Mum this time. 'You know, this came from your family — from your witchy sister and your mother the witch!'

Dottie was angry then. Her voice was icy calm. 'Oh, please, John. You're just frightened because you don't understand. And there is nothing to be frightened of. The girl has her grandmother's extra vision and healing hands, and you have an obligation to acknowledge that and make sure she knows that you love her for who she is. You have an obligation ...'

'*Don't* tell me about my obligations,' he thundered. 'You don't even have children of your own. You've got no right, coming into this house, *my* house, and telling me how to bring up my kids. Theney has nothing wrong with her that hard work and a normal life won't fix. The last thing I'm going to do is acknowledge anything different about her. As far as I am concerned she's just a normal healthy kid going through a stage. You know how girls her age can get, with their heads full of fancy. The only chance she's got of a normal life is if she is normal ...'

Dottie's quiet voice chipped in then. 'John, what you're saying is ridiculous and I'll go because I don't want to cause trouble in the family. But think about my offer ...'

But Dad interrupted her again. 'If you think that I am going to send my daughter to spend the summer with you so you can fill her head with ridiculous notions ... And besides, I need her here. I'm short of help. The hay's nearly ready and we need everybody we can get to help with the baling.'

There was a silence for a moment. I could feel the tension in the room even from behind the closed door, and I hugged my stomach in fear of what would happen next. But Dottie let the moment pass.

'Christine,' she said to my mother, 'please try to talk some sense into your husband, and think about your daughter's happiness. You know where to find me. Make sure she knows as well.'

I heard footsteps coming towards my hiding place, and I ran back to my bedroom so I wouldn't be caught listening.

PROSPECT

By the time you go back upstairs to the bar two things have happened: Aubrey Meadows has disappeared, and the Princess has moved to a table where she is sitting holding hands with someone you have not seen before. She looks happy — you can see a glow about her that wasn't there before.

As you approach, she lets him go and stretches out her hand to you, makes you part of her circle, sprinkles you with magic Princess fairy dust and says, 'And this is my dearest friend, Theney. Theney, I would like you to meet Robert, an old friend of mine I never expected to see again'.

'Pleased to meet you.' You extend your hand.

He murmurs 'Likewise' and shakes it. He seems wary and you wonder what the Princess has told him. Or what he's seen.

The Princess is coquettish now. 'Robert's just been telling me he used to have a crush on me. Weren't you Robert?'

You look at him and believe that this is true. It is clear also that the crush never entirely left him. He has also figured out the lie of the land — he knows that you are designated driver and also protector of the Princess. He perceives the barrier. But you like the warmth of him, and you see the Princess does as well.

'Can I get you a drink?' he offers. You nod and allow yourself a little smile.

His eyebrow questions.

'Shiraz,' you say. 'And then I have to go.' You look meaningfully at the Princess, 'Then *we* have to go'.

The Princess pouts at you and shakes her empty glass at him and he actually looks at you as though for permission, before he agrees to get her another vodka martini and moves towards the bar.

'Isn't he gorgeous?' She's breathless.

'Where's your friend, Aubrey?'

'Oh, he said to say goodbye. You know, he was a little bit upset that you didn't like him. He really liked you.'

'What?'

'He asked if he'd done something wrong. He really liked you.'

You snort. It simply doesn't bear thinking about.

'What do you think of Robert?' she asks.

You settle back in your chair. 'What do you mean, "what do I think?" ' you ask, smiling. You're safe again, in the Princess' problems.

Just two days later, Robert calls the Princess. You know it is Robert because she taps the pre-arranged signal on the pipe that runs along the adjoining wall between your apartments. You hear the 'tap tap tap, pause, tap tap tap' just above your head, as you sit on your sofa and watch the news on your television. You turn and rest your hand on the wall and send her silent thoughts, reminding her to be kind. She protects her private self with cruelty sometimes and you think that Robert does not deserve cruelty. After she has done flirting with him, she calls you and tells you about it. At least you suppose she flirted with him. You've been in her apartment when she does it with the others who call. She only ever admitted doing it once, after you'd shared almost two bottles of Moët. Usually she acts innocent and pretends it's all an accident.

You smile at her voice. The Princess hasn't been this excited on the end of a phone for a long time. 'He called!' she says. And then 'I need you to come to a party with me this weekend.'

'But I was going to San Antonio this weekend ...'

'I know, but couldn't you go some other time? He's asked me to a party, and it's people I don't know. I really like him, but I don't want to go to this party all by myself. I need you to look after me.'

You sigh. She knows the words that work. You can never resist a cry for help.

And you weren't going away for any special event, after all — San Antonio can wait one more weekend. In fact, it's almost a relief to know you have to cancel the trip.

'Which night?' you ask.

'Saturday!' she says. 'I knew you wouldn't let me down.'

'I haven't said I'll come yet.' But you both know you will. This is just the game you play. 'Let me make some calls. I'm not promising anything ...'

'I know, I know. Thank you, Theney.'

DOTTIE'S NOTEBOOK

When I was sixteen my mother died. They let her come home from the hospital, and for days I sat beside her, holding her hand. She was so thin I could see the skull through the paper skin on her face. The hospital had let her come home to die.

She kept her eyes closed and her breathing was so shallow that sometimes I held my own breath until I couldn't stand it any more, trying somehow to force her to breathe deeper. Maybe, I thought, if I transferred the distress my own body felt at the lack of oxygen to her then she would start to breathe properly again, in sympathy or something. But her breaths remained shallow and I was left gasping for air.

'I want her at home,' said Dad, 'so she can look out the window and see the mountains and we can put roses from her own garden in her room. And besides,' said Dad, 'it's a busy time of year. Someone has to run the farm. It's a three-hour drive to the hospital ...'

They sent a nurse out to the farm and I learned how to put the morphine into Mum's arm, with a bag on a stand and a needle in the little white plastic tube taped to her hand.

'You're good at this,' said the nurse.

'I wish I were good at making her better instead of helping her die.'

She looked at me. 'Be strong,' she said. 'Be strong for her. It's a big journey.'

'How did you know that?' I asked.

'What?'

'That it's a journey. Everybody else around here thinks that dying is an ending. You talk about it as though you know different. Dad says I should just get a grip on reality. He says I need to accept that death is the end.'

'Well,' said the nurse. 'You know what you know.'

She was going to say more, I was sure, but Dad came into the room. He could not look at Mum any more. I hadn't even seen him touch her since she came back from hospital this time. He looked as though he was scared of her. His eyes roved around the room, resting on the nurse and on me and on the vase of flowers beside my mother's bed — but never on her face.

'How is she.'

It was not said like a question. His voice was flat and empty. The nurse walked over to him and touched his arm.

'Let me make you a cup of tea, Mr Fairweather. We can talk about my next visit.'

That night I moved my bed into the room with her so I could be close by. I woke in the dark time between night and morning and saw the angel of death standing over her. At first I thought it was Dad. Perhaps he had come quietly into the room and was standing by her bed, finally coming to grips with this thing that was happening. But as my eyes opened properly, I saw that the figure who stood there was not human. It was filled with light and yet, strangely, not radiating — as though the light was turned inwards. The figure was standing over my mother.

I was paralysed as though in a dream, but I knew that it was not a dream. I watched, and somehow knew — my mother was marked. Preparations were being made. I don't remember the angel leaving and I don't remember falling asleep. But when I woke, the room was dark and it was just the two of us in there, Mum and me. I got up and stood by her bed, watching her for a moment. I touched her hand and she turned her head to look at me.

'Theney ...' her voice died away a little after saying my name. She smiled, the first time in months. 'We never talked about your gift. I'm sorry I haven't been much help.' Her voice was so small I could hardly hear it.

'That's okay, Mum ... Is there anything you need?'

'No, love. It's nearly over,' she said.

I knew she was right. I'd known, while holding her hand all those hours that she didn't need what I could give her. I couldn't save her with this gift. It was a strange thing to see her body ravaged by cancer and then to feel when I touched her that she had no fear, no pain in her heart. I felt more fear for her than she did.

When I told my father about the angel, he just scoffed. 'You shouldn't eat so late at night. Did you get up and raid the fridge? When you sleep on a full stomach, it gives you bad dreams. You know that, Theney.'

And when I saw the angel again on the second night I told Dad again. It irritated him, but I thought he ought to know. He was sitting at the kitchen table with a cup of tea in front of him and his head in his hands.

'That's crap!' he said, looking up at me angrily. 'Why don't you just face it, like a normal person. She's dying and … she's dying and …'

He could not go on. And I disobeyed him then, despite myself. I did the thing that made him fear me, the thing he wanted me to never do, never talk about, the thing I kept inside me like a guilty secret. I went to him and sat next to him and put my hand on his heart and cleared away the blockage in there that would not let him cry. I poured my love for him into him, and I took away his fear and he let out a long, shuddering moan, before finally letting go. Big man sobs came breaking out of him, and he buried his face in his rough hands, scarred and calloused from building fences, and chipping thistles and fixing farm machinery. The same hands that gentled horses and pulled burrs from the dogs' ears. The same hands that could pull a lamb from its weakened mother and clean its mouth and nose passages and hold it to its mother's teat, with quiet words and a sort of glow about him. And when he had finished crying he went and sat beside Mum's bed and held her hand in his. He sat with her, like that, until she died, at three in the morning, with him holding one hand, and me on the other side of her, woken just half an hour before by something I

36

could not see and stroking her hair and feeling her slip away.

He could not pretend that I was normal any more, because now he had felt for himself what I could do. He never spoke of it and nor did I, but after that he hardly spoke to me again about anything at all. It was not just that my mother had died. There was no place in his world for what I was. So I lost a mother and a father and gained instead the feeling of aloneness that began to be the flavour of my life.

The next summer, I left home and moved down to the city, to Melbourne, to stay with Dottie.

PROSPECT

On Saturday night, you volunteer to drive. You are not comfortable giving other people control of steering wheels, brakes and accelerators on icy winter streets, particularly on nights like this when there is love in the air and alcohol in nearly every bloodstream. Maybe if you'd grown up in these conditions you would trust more.

Today had been unseasonably warm but now it is so cold outside that the melted snow on the roads has turned to black ice — invisible but deadly. Tonight, Robert and the Princess are happy to give directions from where they sit wrapped around each other in the back seat while you perch up front like a chauffeur. You drive carefully and the two of them make out. You wish you were someone else or somewhere else. You turn the rear-view mirror away so you cannot see them, using the side mirrors instead to check for traffic behind the car. In fact, you look in the side mirrors more than you need to. It keeps your eyes busy, distracts them from the natural consequences of self-pity and an exaggerated sense of loneliness.

After a few missed turns and the occasional double-back because the Princess and Robert, smooching in the back seat, keep losing track of time and space, you finally arrive at the building where they say you should be, just a few blocks from Linklatters. It is large, maybe six stories high and looks less like a home than a factory. You think they must have made a mistake when they finally tell you to stop. There are no lights.

Robert and the Princess get out of the car and run giggling and slipping in the ice to a small dark doorway. 'Come on, Theney!' the Princess beckons.

The door has been jammed open with a stone; Robert pushes it open, then he and the Princess run, still giggling, up the dimly lit stairwell, and you follow, with a sense of foreboding. When they stop outside the door, you suddenly know who lives there. It flashes through your head so certainly that when Aubrey Meadows opens the door you are not surprised. The Princess planned it all along. You can't believe she would set you up like this. She knows you don't …

You hang back a little. Calculating the distance to the car, you wonder briefly about the consequences of running for it, of leaving now. But it's too late.

'Theney, honey,' says the Princess in that Southern drawl again. 'You remember Aubrey.'

'Hi,' you say. And then stupidly, 'Sorry about the other night …' You step forward and put out your hand. He just looks at you and steps back to let you in. You walk past him and into his home, wishing that the floor would swallow you up.

Inside, he takes your coat and you look to the other side of the room and see that the Princess does not need you. She seems to know everybody here. It has only been seconds and she has kissed nearly half the cheeks in the place already. Besides, as you watch her and Robert together you see that she did not need a chaperone, that the two of them have already begun to be something other than just the Princess and Robert. You must have lost your mind to ever think she did. You are here under false pretences. You are seriously angry with her for meddling. It feels as though they are throwing you at this man, and they have no right to do that. You decide to leave at the earliest possible opportunity but in the meantime you will look around. The place is interesting.

He lives alone. You can see that almost immediately, though if pressed you may not be able to say exactly how you know. This is less an apartment than a space, with ceilings maybe five or six metres high. It's what you imagined an artist's loft would be like. One corner of the space has been partitioned off to make two separate rooms, and in the far corner is a circular staircase leading up to a mezzanine floor where you can see the corner of a mattress. The rest of it is open plan, completely. There are plants. There are books. There are CDs by the hundred. A baritone saxophone leans on its stand and a tenor and alto saxophone lie on their sides on shelves near the beaten-up sofa in the corner.

The lower part of one of the walls is covered with sketches, hundreds of them. They seem to be sketches of people but you cannot see the detail from where you sit. High shelves run all around the walls. Two lava lamps. An enormous television sits in one corner and, below it, in the cabinet a serious stereo with a graphic equaliser the likes of which you have never seen. Around it a cluster of people are discussing which CDs to put on next. A keyboard rests on a table beside the stereo; it's covered in sheets of music with scribble all over them. Somebody has been working here. On the lower walls around the television and near the space that serves as a kitchen is such a mix of objects that you cannot see the sense of it. Three different statues of the Madonna — including a phosphorescent-looking one that you suspect would glow in the dark; a rattlesnake skin, thin and delicate like tracing paper; Japanese Kabuki masks; something that looks like Papua New Guinean head dress and a penis sheath, separated by a mounted bird-eating spider, presided over by a crucifix complete with an agonised bleeding Christ looking down in disbelief at the gaping wound in His side.

More people arrive, trickling in the front door. And then you notice that some of them are carrying musical instruments. A double bass has already come in, and a guitar and some African drums. The musical instruments gather in the corner.

A voice you know asks you if you want a drink. It is Lloyd. You look around and grin at him; what relief to find him here.

'Always the bartender. I'd love one. Point me to it. And what are you doing here?'

'Hey, it's Aubrey's party. That's one of my rules. Never miss one of Aubrey's parties.' He puts his arm around your shoulders. 'Come and meet Rosa.' Leonard Cohen moans unrequited passion from the Bose speakers perched in every corner in the room. Lloyd is partnered.

You had no idea. You also had no idea it would kick you like this to find out. You had no idea you gave a damn at all. When you shake Rosa's hand and say hello you see that she glows warm and you can almost see the sparkles playing above her mass of curls. Lloyd is greatly loved. You look at him looking at her and see how he reaches out to her. It kills you.

Armed with vodka and cranberry juice (you need the strength and cleanness of them to help you manage all this danger) you wander around the room with all its noise and revelations, looking for an unobtrusive place to sit. You will finish your vodka and then slip out somehow. It won't be hard. Everyone is drinking and smoking and talking. It will be easy to leave. No one will care. The Princess will understand. Or not. After what she's done by bringing you here, you just don't care.

What you really need is a soft chair and a dim light. All he has are high ceilings, bright lights and hard surfaces with raggedy bits and pieces of furniture thrown in to make the surfaces livable. There is nowhere for a girl to sit and contemplate. In the one corner of the room that has been partitioned off, there are two doors. One leads to the toilet and a constant trickle of people wander in and out. You would have to cross the room to see where the other door leads and you don't want to draw attention to yourself. The only place that seems quiet and removed is the mezzanine with the mattress. It doesn't seem quite right to go into his sleeping space, but the intrusion can be rationalised. Your need to separate from the party is overwhelming.

The coast seems clear and you slip up the stairs and

turn to check. No one has even noticed you are here. It is more than just a sleeping space. It is enclosed on three sides, and he has rugs on the wooden floor, an old wide chair, a reading light and one whole wall of books. You stand in the oasis, sipping your drink. On one wall is a collage of family photos and with a faint but easily ignored sense of invading his privacy, you step over to take a look. They *are* family photos: Aubrey with a woman who looks like she must be his wife — he has his arm around her waist and she is laughing up at him; two little babies; another woman, much older — his mother? Hers? As you look more closely a photo in the centre of the collage catches your eye and stops your breath — it is a photo of Aubrey. His eyes are looking straight at the camera, although his head is half turned. From the photo, he looks at you again, just like he did in the flesh, the first time. Something in his eyes entrances you and you get close enough to look into them. Without thinking, you test the air for the scent of sadness that you know should be there. You wonder what he did to get to a place where he could put such a photo at the very centre of a collage filled with happy family images. And yet, you suddenly realise, you know that the picture makes sense. You wonder if it makes as much sense to him as it does to you.

'Here you are.' His voice behind you makes you jump.

'What?'

'What do you think?'

'I don't ...' you start, feeling a flush of embarrassment. But he doesn't let you finish.

'You do. What do you think?'

You make a snap decision — to be honest and bugger the consequences. You take a breath. 'All these family photos, full of happiness — but this one,' you point, 'it's the most important picture in the whole collage and it's the opposite. You're in a terribly sad place. But you're protecting it as well. You're defiant.' The flush you feel begins at your chest and rises up to your face. 'In the photo I mean.' You flounder. 'I mean in the photo,' and then, idiotically, 'sorry.'

You can see, with some relief, that you haven't upset him, though it almost would have been easier for you if you had. Something about him keeps making you want to run away.

'Come with me,' he says, pointing down the stairs. 'We've nearly run out of beer and I have to get some more before the liquor store closes.'

You follow him down the stairs and to the coat cupboard near the front door. You wait, nervous, while he gets your coat. You think you might need to pee, but you're not sure enough to say anything. He holds your coat open for you before he puts on his own. He takes your gloved hand, which makes you jump again. Together you sneak out the door, escaping the party.

In his car, you don't know what to say. You look out the window.

'Why are you here? Who are you?' he asks.

The questions seem big. You think they demand that you start at the beginning, but the beginning escapes you. The beginning of what? You pretend that he is asking the smaller question.

'The Princess said I should come.'

He looks puzzled. 'The Princess?' and then a gust of laughter. 'Oh, you mean ...! Ha! That's perfect. The Princess. But I don't mean tonight. Why are you in Prospect, Nebraska, of all places? You look more like the type that should be trying to leave.'

'I'm here for work, sort of. I'm supposed to be in San Antonio, in Texas. I was on my way there but I came here first to do some stuff for the company I worked for in Australia. They have an office here. But anyway, that was a little more than a year ago. And here I still am. I think I can find what I need here, when I figure out exactly what that is.'

This is a great deal to have spouted out in one response. You look across at him, but he seems to be concentrating on the road. He says nothing. In the car's dark interior it is impossible to see any reaction on his face. You pull your knees up under your chin.

'Sometimes I think that Prospect chose me. It called and I came. At first I thought I might find some answers here, because I'm sort of starting everything from the beginning, and re-inventing myself. It's so different to anything ...'

Still, he says nothing. Words jumble in your head and you want to be careful to let only the right ones out. You think about the fact that there is so much nothingness here in Prospect. How cold the winters are and how no one knows you. No one knows who you are and what mistakes you've made and what your patterns are, the guilty secret of this gift you do not want. And if you tell him too much, you might reveal the old Theney and give her a foot-hold — the scared Theney who takes

45

people's pain away and who has to run away from the consequences; the Theney who can't find anyone to love, because she's too busy trying to avoid healing people. You can't tell him too much because it would entirely defeat your mission to begin again and exorcise the past.

'I'm a writer,' you begin again. And then you stop again because the conversation that would probably arise if you pursued this would involve you having to admit that you are not just a writer; you are a technical writer, which means nothing to most people, and you write memories in your notebook, which is not so unusual. By some measuring devices you are not a writer at all. You do not want him to think you are just a dreamer, a wannabe writer.

'I work in I.T. For a computer software company.'

You look at him again, without turning your head and you can still see the light around him. Somehow, your real question behind all this sneaks out before you can stop it.

'Why are you paying me so much attention?'

He does not answer immediately. In the dark you feel that your neck and face are flushed again. He keeps doing this to you. It was a question you should not have asked.

'My cousin ...,' he says, pausing, choosing his words carefully. 'We talked about you. Do you believe in angels?'

The question could only be taken seriously by the sort of person who feels and occasionally sees auras, and who thinks that a person can escape their demons with an airline ticket and an extended stay in a town in the Mid-

West of America that no one has ever heard of. So you take it seriously.

'I don't know what to say,' is all you can think to say, as he pulls into a parking space outside the door of the liquor store.

He opens your door and closes it behind you after you have stepped out onto the snow. He ushers you inside the shop and you watch him get a case of beer, a bottle of vodka. You watch him as he decides he actually needs two bottles of vodka. You stand at the counter silently, hoping that if you watch him carefully enough you will understand. But it is too early for understanding. He is still a stranger and it will take more time before you know what things about him will end up being significant.

The person behind the counter is of unkempt indiscriminant gender, but when she speaks, you hear that she is a woman. She has just a couple of teeth, in the front. She knows Aubrey. 'How are they treating you?' she asks, looking not directly at him, but to the side of his head.

'They're leaving me be tonight,' he says, and looks at you sidelong, as though caught out.

The toothless woman looks directly at you and you hesitate a smile. 'Demons,' she says. But her face shows no expression. You see that she does not even see surfaces. She looks right inside of things. She looks at you a minute longer than is comfortable for you, then looks away. An almost imperceptible shake of the head.

Aubrey picks up the case and you pick up the vodka

bottles. You follow him out. At the doorway you turn, for some reason and look at her again.

She was waiting for you to turn. 'You didn't come such a long way for nothing,' she cackles. 'What do you think you're here for?' There's a bubble of spit on her bottom lip. 'He knows. But he doesn't know he knows. And you haven't even got a clue, even though you see it all.' Her stare pierces you. 'You see it, don't you, all around them, just like me.'

You cannot meet her eye. This is too unexpected. You push the door so roughly that you nearly end up sprawled on the ground outside, but somehow you recover and the door shuts hard behind you with the tinkle of a bell and an echo of the old woman's cackle.

In the car again, you turn to Aubrey. 'What …? Who …?' He shakes his head. 'Don't ask. I don't know.' He drives you back to his house in silence.

Outside his door, you stand and look at each other. Finally, he says 'Can I call you next week? Would you come out to dinner with me?'

You shake your head and take your hand out of your glove to touch his cheek, a gesture that surprises you because you have trained yourself not to touch. Halfway to his cheek your hand hesitates as you realise what you are doing, but it would be too weird to stop now so you touch his stubble and see a smile light him up. He reaches up to touch your hand but you pull it away just in time. You put your glove back on and say a quiet goodnight, then walk away up the street, forgetting that your car is in the other direction.

As you walk away, he shouts out 'Will you come and

hear me play? Do you like jazz?' You ignore him. A minute later the door to his house shuts. You hear it click as he goes inside.

A little way up the street you find a low fence to sit on and then straight away you feel sick so you throw up under a bush and then wipe your mouth and sit for a while longer in the icy night, which has suddenly turned black and brittle. It takes a long time before you are confident you can move without throwing up again. You cannot even feel the cold. Perhaps it was the vodka.

DOTTIE'S NOTEBOOK

At nineteen I was living in Dottie's house in Melbourne, though she was hardly there. She had a home in San Antonio, Texas, and she only spent three months a year in Australia. Of course I went to her when I ran away, before I began to understand that who I am refuses to be left behind.

'You can't hide from who you are,' warned Dottie as she handed me a cup of tea in a cup covered in yellow roses. 'Theney, you have to find a way to walk in the world with your head held high, or you'll find all the stuff you're trying to bury sneaks up behind you afterwards and bites you on the behind.'

'Love,' and she touched my hand. 'It's not your father's fault he doesn't understand, but it's not your fault either. Nobody's at fault, but you have to face the truth about your gift and find a way to live with it.'

'I'm never going to do it again,' I said. 'I haven't done it since Mum died. Perhaps I can't any more.' I looked into my tea. 'I hope not. You said it goes away sometimes.'

She looked at me then, in that way she had that made me feel like she was reading my mind or my heart or some secret deep inside me, then she shook her head. 'No Theney. It hasn't gone, my love. And I'm serious. Face it, or it will turn against you, eat you up inside, make you lonely.' She touched my cheek. 'You're a precious speck, Theney. Learn to love who you are.'

Dottie had to come back to America — to San Antonio, of course, not Prospect. I doubt she'd ever been here, or even heard of it for that matter. No one has. She gave me a present on the morning she left.

'It's a notebook, a journal,' she said as I unwrapped it, and she seemed nervous, worried that I would not like it. 'I know you're unhappy. I know you don't want this thing you have. You need to talk to someone about it,' she touched my arm, 'and we both know there aren't many people you can tell.' She smiled gently and touched my face in that way she had. 'So write it down, Theney my love. Just writing it down will help you understand. You can stay here as long as you like,' she said. 'It will be good to have someone in the house. And don't just sit inside and read, like you normally do. Why don't you get a job while you decide what you want to do with your life? Learn to type or something. Go and see what you can find. Get out of the house. Meet some people.' She kissed me on the cheek. 'I'll be back as soon as I can,' she said.

I opened that notebook so many times, touched its empty pages, held it up to my face and smelled the clean emptiness of it. And then closed it without writing a single word. I didn't know where to begin. I didn't see the point.

PROSPECT

He does call, despite the fact that you did not give him your number. When you see his name and number appear on your caller ID box, you do not pick up the phone. The Princess then calls, which confirms your suspicions that she was where he got your number. She's calling to check. Again, you do not pick up the phone.

Sunday passes, and on Monday you cannot face going to the office, so you stay in bed all day, with a book. Escaping in the pages of Kerouac's *The Subterraneans*. Reading the semi-autobiographical output of a gifted life that seems even more confusing to Kerouac than your own seems to you is solace, in a way, for what ails you.

On Monday afternoon, the phone rings and the caller ID box once again helps you decide whether to answer it. It is someone from the office, probably your boss. Senior Vice President of Websites. His real title sounds much more important — resonating with the weight of responsibility carried by a man in charge of internal and external corporate communications. You think Senior VP, Websites, sounds much better, and it makes him laugh, besides. He likes your wacky Australian sense of humour and it amuses you to play along. You pick up the phone.

'Theney here.'

It is him. 'Hi Theney, this is Terry,' he says. 'I notice you haven't been in today. Anything wrong?'

He's such a sweetheart. You explain your problem. 'I have something gastric.'

'Oh, dear,' he says. 'Do you need a doctor?'

'I already went,' you lie. 'It feels like heartburn, but it's actually something much worse.' You feel quite clever for the half-truth of this. Heartburn. Much worse.

'Okay,' he says. 'Take care of you. Let me know if you need anything.'

Another day passes, and another. Then, exhausted by your own company, you go to Linklatters and Lloyd is behind the bar.

'Theney!' He seems genuinely pleased. He wants to know how you are doing. He senses something's not right. 'Are you all right?' he asks, looking closely at your face.

'Sure,' you say as you raise your glass of Shiraz in a salute.

It is quiet at Linklatters. Wednesday nights are never very busy.

'You eating tonight?' he asks.

'What's the soup?'

'New England Clam Chowder or Spicy Tomato.'

'I'll think about it,' you say.

Lloyd hesitates, as though not sure, but finally speaks. 'He's okay, you know. He's a good guy. Just had a run of bad luck.'

You must have inadvertently given him some sort of look, because he raises his hands in defence and apologises for sticking his nose in where it's not wanted. 'I'm sorry,' he says. 'I'll keep my nose out of it.'

You take a swallow of Shiraz. 'How do you know him?'

'He's my cousin.'

'Oh.' You remember something. 'Was it you who said that thing about me being an angel?'

'He told you that?'

You nod.

'Lord, that man has *no* idea.'

'Was it you?'

He nods, after a moment's hesitation.

'What did you mean?' you ask.

'There's something about you …' He hesitates. 'This is going to sound crazy. And it's only my opinion.'

'Go on. I understand.'

'Well, you're missing something. Like you're lost. I see you in here, and don't get me wrong,' he raises his hands again in defence, 'I like to see you. But I think you're only here because you're lost.' He moves to the little dishwasher behind the bar and takes a tray of glasses out. He picks up a tea towel and starts to polish them and put them away, one by one. 'There's something good about you. He needs something good. There's something lost about you. He could help you find your way. You could be his angel. He could be yours.' A shrug of his shoulders. 'That's all.'

A customer down at the other end of the bar yells 'Hey, Lloyd'. He pats you on the shoulder and heads down the bar to take the guy's order.

You down your drink and leave. Driving home, you find it difficult to see the road. As you put the key in your door you change your mind and decide you need to see the Princess.

DOTTIE'S NOTEBOOK

I tried to bury who I was, with what seemed like reasonable success. I succeeded in that I managed to avoid using the gift, or writing in the notebook Dottie had given me. But I didn't know what I wanted to do with my life. I would have read all day if I could have. Reading had always been my preferred method of escape, but a farm upbringing had given me a punitive work ethic so I bought myself a Learn to Type book and practised on Dottie's golfball typewriter until I could write *"The quick brown fox jumps over the lazy dog"* at the rate of thirty words a minute — the bare minimum acceptable to the employment agencies I had called.

I had no qualifications, no office experience. Baling hay or throwing fleeces were useless skills to have in Melbourne. So I bought a suit with some of the money that Dottie had given me to live on, and started knocking on doors, with my brand new résumé and my heart in my mouth. I couldn't type fast enough to be classified as a typist and I had never used a word processor or computer so they couldn't give me a word processing job, but eventually an agency took pity on me and placed me in a short-term job as a receptionist in a doctor's surgery.

It nearly killed me. I suppose you would think that people coming to a doctor's surgery might be suffering merely from some physical ailment. I had thought that what I had seen of my mother was what I could expect from most sick people. Her body was sick but her mind and her heart were not, and she needed me less than my father did, even though he was in perfect physical health. It was the same for all the farm people I knew. But the connection between physical illness and heart sickness was stronger in the city.

What I learned as a doctor's receptionist in Melbourne is that for many people their physical ailments are simply a manifestation of some other type of disease. I learned never to touch, even though I had a compelling need to respond to what I felt. And even though I worked there for some weeks, I never became desensitised. Perhaps only one in twenty people was not suffering some terrible sadness or heart's dis-ease that was a root cause of their exterior illness. People came in with all sorts of ailments, but I could see their lights were patchy around different parts of their bodies and I soon learned some patterns. Stomach and digestion problems were often caused by terrible emotional blockages around hearts and belly buttons. Colds and bronchitis showed up as patchy spots around the throat — less to do with the actual throat than with an inability to communicate some problem and thereby release it. Those were weeks when I learned more about my sight than I had ever realised was possible, and yet, after the first few impulses, I managed not to touch anyone. In that way, at least, it was a horrible experience. I felt the need to help. The pull towards this sickness was compelling and resisting the pull made me feel as though I was betraying some obligation.

Three things stopped me. One was fear. The doctor's waiting room was like a magnet for heartache, disguised as other things. I was sure that if I let even a trickle of this reservoir into myself, the flow would grow and grow until I was overwhelmed by it. I was sure I would have drowned in it.

And the second thing was that what I had seen before, as a child and later on, was also true here. If I touched someone with the express purpose of taking that thing away from them, they could feel it. The first response to my gift was always fear. The eyes would widen, the heart-rate increase, and something would tighten around whatever lump or blockage I had seen in them. The first response was to protect their heartache, keep it safe, even though it made them miserable!

And finally, the hardest thing was what I'd seen in my father and in others I had touched. Even if I could put my hand on someone's heart and take their pain away, they simply made more. I wasn't healing anybody — just providing temporary relief. The pain, or sadness, was generated by something I couldn't touch — something only they could heal, or that could only be healed with some other gift that I did not have.

Dottie was in America and I had trouble talking to her about my gift on the phone so I couldn't ask her for advice. This was my first job and I wanted her to be

58

proud of me. I was determined not to fail. I had something to prove — to myself and to Dottie, to my father, to the world.

I was coping. I built walls. I retreated to the filing compactus when things got really bad, but overall, I could honestly say that things were going all right. Until one day I met Rosie and her mother, and everything fell to pieces.

PROSPECT

The Princess always has champagne. And strawberries. And water crackers. Cream cheese, smoked salmon. And tiny little capers in a jar. She's pleased to see you, even at this time of night.

'Can I hang out here for a while?' is all you need to say.

She grabs your hand and pulls you inside. There is nothing for it but to fill the champagne flutes and put some music on the stereo and indulge in a little girl talk. You lean back onto the plush cushions she has on her couch. She leans conspiratorially towards you.

'So ... When are you and Aubrey going out on a date?'

'Never,' you retort. That is not what this is about.

'Why, what happened?'

'Nothing.'

'Theney, he likes you.'

'Should I go out with someone just because he likes me? Or am I allowed to choose someone I like in return?'

'How can you know whether you like him or not; you haven't given him a chance.'

'Well, how can he like me — he's only just met me,

too.' You feel quite proud of the logic of this. You celebrate by dropping a strawberry in your champagne, to reward yourself with later.

'Theney, how long have I known you?'

You snort. 'As long as I've known you, I suppose.'

She leans back on the sofa and stretches her arm out behind her, looking ready to miaow. 'I'm serious. Theney, you saw through me straight away, and it takes most people months, if at all. You never believed that I was the silly thing that everyone else believes I am.'

'How much have you drunk?' you ask suspiciously.

'Stop,' she says, putting her hand on your arm. 'I'm really serious. We've never talked about this and I don't want to intrude but I have to say this. You see to the truth of people, but you also have a sort of blindness. It's like you're lost ...'

'What's this "lost" bullshit I keep hearing ...'

She looks hurt. 'Theney,' she says, 'What did I say ...'

You shake your head and put your glass down. You have lost interest in drinking. 'It's okay,' you try to reassure her. 'But I haven't been feeling right recently. I just want to be left alone. I think I'd better go.'

'Let him ask you. Say yes. Please, Theney.'

You shout 'Why?!' She jumps back and you try to calm down, try to explain. 'Why should I go out with him? Why should I go on a date? Dating scares the willies out of me! I won't go. I want to meet someone and have something happen naturally, or not at all. Dating is ...'

The words will not come out, but you know what you want to say. And she, who seems to love the ritual, may never understand. A date, you'd learned, was where you circled him; he circled you; questions asked — what do you do? Which church are you? Are you alone? You rent, or own? And then afterwards maybe the two of you decide what you will call this. Is it an isolated date that ends here, or will you try another evening out, a "second date" and then perhaps a third, to find out more? Perhaps you will create a little pattern, a secret language. Perhaps you'll start to smile (or frown) when thinking of him and the funny way he sucks in his cheek before he answers your questions. Perhaps you'll spend enough time with him to know, without thinking too hard, whether he breaks or cuts his dinner roll and what music he plays in his car when you're not there (and you know this because you hear it before he reaches out to turn it down when he starts the car after picking you up as a gentleman should).

No, a date is what you do, all clammy nervousness, a parody of yourself and not really truly who you are; a date is how you test the waters and you wish there were no need of that. You want to be on this side of that experience, alone, or on the other side and partnered. You cannot stand the thought of what you have to do to get from one side to the other.

'Dating is nobody's idea of a good time,' she says gently. 'But you can make it fun. Just don't take it too seriously. He really wants to meet up with you, and I think it would be a good idea. You're always looking after me. Take my advice just this once.'

You are silent. It isn't just the horror of dating. You could almost give it a try if that was all it was.

'Theney?' She touches your arm. 'There is something

else about Aubrey.' She hesitates. 'He lost his wife a couple years ago. She drove her car into the river. They had twin babies, nearly a year old, and she had them in the car with her. They all died. It really messed with his mind.'

'Oh God.' You shake your head and hug your knees. You knew there was something. She hugs you around the shoulders then gets up to refill the champagne glasses. 'But you're my friend,' she says. 'I'll do what you ask.'

An hour later the two of you have rolled up her loungeroom rug and are dancing to Abba's *Greatest Hits* and singing all the words and the champagne has nearly gone.

Two hours later you are back in your apartment and half way up the stairs to your bedroom, sitting on the sixth step with your head and arms resting on the ninth step, quietly crying and telling your sorrow to the carpet.

DOTTIE'S NOTEBOOK

It was a Thursday. Nothing special. The usual stream of colds and flus, haemorrhoids and lesions, heartaches and loneliness.

And then, at about ten a.m. when I was thinking I should make a coffee, I suddenly felt it. I looked up to where Rosie and her mother had just walked in through the door to the waiting room; what I felt from them hit me so deeply that a wave of nausea washed over me from my toes right up to the top of my head and for a moment I could not even speak.

They walked over to the reception desk, and the mother said to me. 'We have an appointment. My little girl fell over and I think she broke her arm.' I managed to stand up and look over the edge of the reception desk, down to where Rosie stood. She was about six, I guessed, and her left arm was in a makeshift sling.

Something was terribly wrong here. I knew immediately that Rosie had not fallen over. Her light was clear, bright and strong, but there was a dark patch right over her heart, and I could feel her confusion and her sense of isolation like a membrane, enclosing her and suffocating her. And I could feel the mother's pain as well, though not as clear. There is something sharp about the pain that children feel. My hand started moving towards the two of them, on its own. It took all my strength to act normally.

'Take a seat,' I said. 'The doctor will be with you in a few minutes.'

After seeing them, the doctor told Rosie that she had to have an X-ray. There was a radiologist down the hall. I would usually just give people directions when they had to go down there, but this time, I decided to take them myself.

'I'll show you where to go,' I said.

I put my hand out, and Rosie grabbed it. 'My name is Rosie,' she said. When I felt her touch, I lurched and had to grab the wall for support. The mother looked at me strangely.

I led them into the reception area of the radiologist's rooms. There was nobody there. 'Wait here,' I said. 'Someone will be here shortly.' I didn't want to leave. 'Would you like a glass of water or something?' I asked.

'No thanks,' said the mother. Rosie wouldn't let go of my hand. I looked across at the mother. She was frowning.

'Rosie, let go of the lady's hand,' she snapped. 'She's busy.'

'It's all right,' I said, on an impulse. 'I'll get some water for her. She can come with me. We'll only be a minute.'

The mother nodded reluctantly. 'Be a good girl,' she

said to Rosie, and there was something menacing in her voice. I felt Rosie's little hand tighten around mine.

At the water fountain I tried to get Rosie to let go. 'I just have to put some water in one of those little plastic cups,' I smiled at her. 'I need both my hands for a moment.'

Rosie shook her head. And then she moved my hand towards her heart. She looked up at me and asked, 'Will you make it go away?'

'What?' I shook my head, confused. I squatted down beside her. 'What did you say?'

'Can you make it go away? Make it go away. My sister used to make it go away for me but she's gone now. You do it like this. I'll show you.' And she put my hand on her chest, just above her heart, holding my gaze the entire time.

'How did you know?'

'I can see,' she said. 'You look the same as my sister.'

So I did it. In front of the water fountain, in clear view if someone had happened to walk in, I put my hand on her heart and felt it begin. I watched her light brighten and felt all these things a child should never have to feel accumulate in the space behind my heart, and in return I gave her strength and love to put in the space behind hers.

When we were done, she put her good arm around my neck and hugged me. 'I love you,' she whispered in my ear, and held my hand all the way back to the room where here mother waited and fidgeted nervously.

'I hope you were a good girl,' said the mother in a shrill voice as we walked back into the room.

I held out the plastic cup. 'Here's some water,' I said. 'In case you change your mind.'

I was too tired to do more. 'I have to go back to my desk now,' I said. 'Goodbye Rosie.'

Later, I asked the doctor about them. 'That little girl, Rosie. What's really going on there?'

The doctor looked at me sharply. 'What do you mean?'

'She didn't fall. She's being hurt by someone she loves.'

'Can you prove it?'

'No. I know it's true though.'

The doctor was not an unkind person. She was just busy. 'Well,' she said. 'Rosie does have a lot of accidents. If she comes in again, I'll look into it.'

But she didn't come in again. She died the following week of complications arising from internal injuries she sustained when she fell off a swing in her local park.

And I resigned from my job as a medical receptionist.

PROSPECT

Eventually you have to go back to work. If nothing else, it serves as a distraction. Work usually manages to save you from this thing you carry around with you. Work and reading. But while reading only offers a temporary escape, the demands of work are such that you can forget — for hours at a time — the problems that arise from seeing more in people than the surfaces they choose to show the world.

Your technical writing job eventually led you to the Internet, and when it took off, so did your career. You love the challenge of researching information that is basically boring, and making it into something that stops people moving on to another web page … for just three more seconds. That really does the job for you. 'Rolls your socks down,' as Lloyd would say.

'Work' at the moment, has a name. It is called project *Arachne*. It used to be called project *Athena* but thankfully the people in charge changed the name. They said it had nothing to do with the fact that your real name is Athena, but even so, it was with some relief that you read the announcement of the change of name in the company newsletter. It felt weird to be working on a project with your own name. For one thing, you were not entirely sure you wanted the close association between a project at work and your identity as an individual. It made it sound as though the project was yours, or that you belonged to the project.

Once, before they changed the name, you were in Linklatters explaining to Lloyd that it upset you how the corporate world borrowed myths and icons from ancient culture and subverted them, sometimes erroneously, to their own purposes — purposes with limited meaning in the wider scheme of things.

'Lloyd,' you had said, 'It's only a freaking website. Why didn't they just call it 'Project Website' or something? What is the point, exactly, of calling it Athena? *Athena*! Spare me. Given the actual myth, they're consigning this website to a life of mediocrity inflated by an overstated sense of self-importance.' This was in itself an overstatement, but you were making a point.

Lloyd just raised one eyebrow and checked the glass he was polishing, holding it up to the light. 'Listen to yourself, Theney,' he said with a smile. 'So much anger. Are you sure you're not just upset they've used your name?'

You frisbeed a coaster in his direction and he ducked so it ended up hitting the back of the waitress standing at the cash register behind him. At this point the conversation had ended, interrupted by the man beside you. You'd been expecting him to say something for a while. He had that look about him. A man with more than his fair share of chat-up lines. There was also something about him that made you uneasy, although you couldn't pinpoint why. He wasn't to be trusted.

'I'll bet you vote Democrat,' he said.

'I beg your pardon?'

'Your ideas,' he said, extending his hand, 'are quite left wing. Like your hairstyle.'

Your hair was short at the moment, and you'd told the hairdresser to give it a purple rinse and cut it so it looked raggedy. One of your regular attempts to disguise your boring straight brown hair and turn it into something interesting.

'Right.' You reached your hand out to meet his, because it would be terribly rude not to. 'You don't muck around, do you. Straight in, boots and all. But you're right. If I could vote here, it probably would be Democrat.'

'I love your accent,' he says. 'You know, I was in Melbourne, Australia recently on business.'

'Good for you,' then relenting, 'Did you have a good time there?'

'I sure did. I think it's a beautiful city. Very European. I was working with this guy Dave. Dave MacAuley …' He was waiting for you to acknowledge something. You nodded, encouraging. And wondering *'left-wing hair?'*

'I thought you might know him. He works in web technology. Quite well known in his field …'

Lloyd snorted, unsuccessfully stifling a laugh. He had heard this sort of thing almost as many times as you had — along the lines of 'I have a couple of friends who live in Australia … can't remember exactly where … their name is Smith, I think. Do you know them?'

'No, sorry, never heard of him. But I've been here a few months, you know, so maybe he wasn't so well known in Australia when I was there.' You wanted to add a sarcastic 'There are only about twenty million of us, you idiot' but decided instead to get up and leave. You had drunk enough, and needed to get home. Perhaps there would be something to watch on cable.

'What did you mean about mediocrity … you know … the Athena thing?' he asked, before you had managed to gather yourself and get out of your seat.

You explained while taking money out of your purse to put on the bar: 'Well Athena invented weaving, right, and she was the goddess of weaving and handicrafts, amongst other things. And there was this peasant, Arachne, who thought she was the best goddamn weaver around, and she challenged Athena to a weaving contest. She actually did quite a good job, much better tapestry than Athena's apparently. Well Athena was a bit of a pain in the arse whenever anyone showed her up — particularly mere mortals. She turned Arachne into a spider — using disrespect as her excuse — hence Arachnids, the spider family.

So why name a web project after the lesser of the weavers? Sure, she invented weaving. No one doubts that, but it's such a knee-jerk reaction to name a web project after her. If you want to create a quality website, and you have to invoke an ancient Greek myth, why not call it Arachne, since she made the better tapestry and she demonstrated guts and initiative, and an ability to be true to herself, despite the risk.'

'Huh,' he said. 'Very interesting.'

'Well,' you said. 'It was lovely chatting. Say hi to Dave. Me and my left-wing hair are going home.'

'You're a very interesting woman.'

'Yeah, in a twisted, sick sort of a way. See you.' And blowing a kiss to Lloyd, 'Ciao, Lloyd,' you're out the door.

And work is also a good way of keeping you grounded, making sure you don't get too separated from reality despite your extrasensory perception and the temptation to live between the pages of books. The next day you went into work and you were called into the office of the Senior Vice-President, Websites.

'Morning, Terry. You asked to see me?'

'Athena, we've got someone new here from the Melbourne office who's interested in seeing more of what you do. Apparently he's been hearing good things.'

Shit. You knew who it was before he sauntered in the door.

'Theney, this is Bill Roberts.'

'Bill. Pleased to meet you.' You put out your hand to him for the second time.

'Likewise.' He shakes your hand, not giving the game away. Or had he already?

'Bill's been working with the new Asia Pac Knowledge Management team in the Melbourne office, including Dave MacAuley, the guy in charge there. Dave's only been with the company a month, you probably wouldn't have met him when you worked in Melbourne. They're thinking of making some changes. Will you show him what we do from this end?'

'Sure … Absolutely.'

Outside Terry's office, before you'd taken more than a few steps towards your own desk, Bill asked you, out of the blue, 'Why are you here, Theney, in the middle of nowhere?'

'I've got a couple of answers, depending on why you want to know. Is this to do with my left-wing hair, or something else?'

'I see I've pressed a button.'

'It just seemed a funny thing to say.'

'I meant no offence. I'd heard about you, you know. From our people in Melbourne.'

'What did you hear?'

'Good things. Interesting things.'

'Like?'

'Does it matter?' He seemed to be toying with you.

'No. But the fact that you're having so much trouble telling me ...'

'I heard some stories. I heard that you're ... gifted.'

'As in "school for the gifted"?'

'No,' he laughed. 'I mean ... You know what I mean.'

'I might, but I don't see why I should stick my neck out if you're not prepared to.'

'Fair enough. I'd like to hear more about it, though, if you ever feel inclined.'

'I won't,' you said shortly.

'Does Terry know about your *special* skills?' he asked with a smile.

'I don't know. Why don't you ask him?' you said, trying to smile back. A wave of panic washed through you.

DOTTIE'S NOTEBOOK

Dottie came home within a week of my call, although I partly wished she hadn't. I didn't want to cause trouble, but I seemed to do it without even trying. In her loungeroom, I told her what had happened and she sighed.

'I know you feel bad about Rosie, but Rosie didn't die because of you. And maybe you gave her something wonderful before she died, something that nobody else could have given her. I can't answer those questions for you; you have to find a way to do that for yourself. Theney, this is your world too and there's a place for you in it, if you can only find it. This journey that you're on, this thing you call your life, is *yours*, Theney. And you need to *make* it yours.

'I have some friends with their own business and they need someone in the office. They're a software house. They're good people. It might be something for you to do, while you figure things out.'

'A software house?'

'They write software, Theney, for computers. Well, for accountants actually, but it's loaded onto computers. But none of that matters. They need someone at the front desk, and I think you'd be perfect. Until you figure out what you really want to do.'

I must have had some sort of look on my face, because she said, kindly, 'You *will* figure things out, Theney, love. Don't worry. I'll call them this afternoon. We'll get you started.'

I don't know what Dottie said about me to Helena, her friend who owned the company, but I ended up joining them as a receptionist, and it became another way that Dottie blessed me.

'Theney, this is Helena. Helena, Theney.'

Helena took my hand in both of hers and seemed to somehow clasp and shake it at the same time. I saw her light was clear and bright and I felt my spirits lift with her touch. 'Welcome aboard, Theney. You're going to save us in our hour of need.' She turned to Dottie. 'Does she know what she has?'

Dottie smiled. 'She's figuring it out.'

In the end we saved each other. Starting me at reception, Helena gave me little writing and research jobs to do as well, and when the business began to grow, she put me onto bigger writing tasks — brochures, product information, presentations for new clients. I met other employees and had to deal with people who came in the front door, but I learned to put up barriers. I could still see the light in people, sense their sadnesses, their joys and desires — but I didn't touch them and I didn't take them on. Sometimes I felt the urge to reach out and touch, but I resisted. I had a quiet, lonely life, living only for the visits home that Dottie made every couple of months, on breaks from her life in San Antonio.

One day Helena called me into her office. 'I want to talk to you Theney,' she said. 'I don't want to lose you on the front desk, but ...' and I braced myself to be fired, imagined calling Dottie to explain, 'there's an opening in our technical writing team and I thought it might be a good idea for you to give it a go.'

It took a minute. 'I beg your pardon?' I asked from within the imagined telephone call to Dottie.

'We'd like you to join the technical writing team.'

'But I like my job. I love it. It hasn't even been two years. Have I done something wrong?'

'No, of course not, and I don't really want to lose you from the front desk. You've been great. But I can't see you being happy there forever, and this is an entry-level position that's come up. I really think you should give it a try.' She leaned forward. 'You've been doing some great work with those brochures and product descriptions. That's why I thought of you.'

'I like doing those,' I admitted.

'Do you know what makes you good at them?' she asked me, leaning forward a little.

'Not really, I hadn't thought about it.' I remembered what she'd said to Dottie when I first began, *Does she know what she has?*, and prepared to deal with whatever questions she might ask. I wanted to keep my gift buried. I didn't want to look at it. It was nobody else's business.

'You have a sensitivity to what we're trying to say, and a wonderful ability to target the information exactly right,' she said. 'It's a gift.'

I braced myself in case there was more, but all she said was 'Will you give it a go?'

I nodded, relieved.

'Great,' she said. 'You understand that you need to get proper training, don't you?'

'I don't ...' you began.

'There are courses you can do part time,' she said. 'I'll help you get enrolled, and we'll give you time off for study and exams. That's one of the conditions of this offer. You need to get a degree.' She reached across and touched my hand and I felt calmer. 'Let's introduce you to the team then,' she smiled.

When I got home, I called Dottie. 'They've promoted me,' I said. 'I'm a technical writer now.'

'Well done, Theney, my love' she said. 'That's wonderful news.'

I decided on the spur of the moment not to tell her how frightened I had felt when Helena started talking about the gift. I knew I would only get a lecture.

PROSPECT

On Thursday, Aubrey calls again. This time you pick up.

'It isn't too late for you, is it?' he asks.

'Too late?'

'I know you probably have to go to work in the morning.'

'Yes. But I can talk for a little while.'

'I just wanted to say hi, I guess,' he said.

'That's nice. How did your party end up?'

'The usual way, you know, a few hangers on still there at four in the morning.' A silence and then he speaks again. 'I wanted to talk about us.'

'There's an us?'

'I just don't want you getting any ideas about me.'

'Like what kind of ideas?'

'Like that you could ever change me or that we could ever be together in a normal way.'

'Why would I want to change you? And what do you mean by normal?'

'You answer everything I say with a question. It's very annoying.'

'I don't mean to be annoying. But you called me and

you're obviously trying to tell me something, but I don't understand what you're talking about.'

'I'm a musician. That's important to me. I have to live my life a certain way. I'm trying to tell you not to get too attached to me.'

'Okay, then. I won't.'

'I hate the way women always try to change you. I can't bear to be manipulated.'

'Okay.'

'They get their claws in and then they want to marry you and you're never sure if they love you or not — because they're such good liars. Women lie all the time. And besides, I'm too old for you.'

'It sounds like you're trying to talk yourself out of something.'

'I just don't want you to think that I could ever fall in love with you.'

'Hey, you called me. Not the other way around.'

'I just wanted to tell you, you know, be careful. And right now I can't afford to get involved. If I start being happy now, my music will suffer. When I'm happy, it doesn't sound the same.'

'So you think we would be happy, do you?'

'There you go again with your questions. I asked you not to do that.'

'No, you said it was annoying. You didn't ask me to stop. And even if you did ask me, I probably wouldn't. I'm a woman, remember. I'm supposed to be annoying.'

'You're enjoying this, aren't you?'

You laugh. 'Just a little bit.'

He changes tack suddenly. 'I want to know more about you. Tell me about yourself.'

'I thought we already did that, in your car the other night. And if I tell you too much you might fall in love with me and then you'd be in trouble, wouldn't you.'

'No, I want to find out more. And don't make fun of me, I'm serious about what I said.' He pauses as if deciding whether to keep talking or hang up. He changes the subject instead. 'I saw you looking at my books when you were in my bedroom. What are you reading at the moment?'

'I always have a few books on the go. But right now, I guess I'm hooked on the Beats. Kerouac and all those dudes. Yeah, Kerouac. I'm into him now.'

'Why Kerouac? He was a punk.'

'How can you say that?'

'Because it's true.'

You say nothing.

'Theney?'

'I'm deciding whether to bite.'

'Well,' says Aubrey, 'That confirms it.'

'What?'

'You'll probably never be happy.'

'Why? How do you know?'

He hesitates. 'You think too much.'

'You sound just like my father. What are you reading, Aubrey?'

'I'm reading about angels. And I've started sketching again — I used to draw a lot when I was a kid, you know, before I started with the music. And all I want to do right now is draw angels. You make me think of angels, you know.'

You feel a shiver up your spine, for no apparent reason. How does he keep doing that, touching you in places that no one is supposed to be able to see?

DOTTIE'S NOTEBOOK

And I was safe for six years, using my gift only to find ways to coax information from the heads of the people whom I learned to call 'Subject Matter Experts'. Everything went smoothly as I learned my trade, until somebody had the brilliant idea of having me work with Daniel, or more precisely, Daniel's documents.

Daniel was revered in the company. In fact, I had heard, there was nobody like him in the industry. He had an IQ of 175, rumour had it. Rumour also had it that he wrote the company's main software product on his own, after hours; and yet, the document he'd written about it, that was supposed to describe how it worked, was completely incomprehensible to anybody else. I, along with everybody else in the company, had heard the rumour that he was being paid one hundred and sixty dollars an hour. And if he left the company — or Heaven forbid, was hit by a bus or something — the company would have been, we'd heard, totally exposed. A piece of corporate jargon that seemed, in context, to mean 'up shit creek without a paddle'. Daniel's precious head held just about all the company's knowledge about the software they built.

I was expected to reduce the risk of exposure by documenting his knowledge. Somebody had told somebody that I could write, and that I was good with people, and so here I was, being fed to the lions. All in the name of reducing exposure. And if I failed, it was no great loss, because I was relatively junior, and only a technical writer. A non-critical casualty.

I went to see Helena. 'I'm not sure. I don't know if I can do this.'

'We have complete faith in you,' she said.

I thought perhaps they knew something I didn't know. Perhaps Daniel had a predilection for country girls with straight brown hair. Or something. But here I was, infiltrating, helping to reduce the potential exposure to loss, should Daniel take it into his precious head to up and leave.

He was very sensitive to cold, was Daniel. Just before I was assigned to do his documents, in the middle of one of the hottest Februaries on record, the thermostat on the air-conditioning unit that serviced our floor went haywire, and kept the temperature at twenty degrees Celsius. We knew this because Daniel measured the temperature at a number of points around the floor at different times of day. He sat at his desk with a jumper on and a towel draped around his shoulders to keep him warm. He sent out bitter, twisted emails to the administrative staff, who immediately dropped everything to run around in ever-diminishing circles to try to solve the problem.

'The temperature is unacceptable,' he wrote. 'I cannot work like this.'

We had all heard that the company nearly broke the lease because the building manager said he couldn't get a new thermostat in to fix the air-conditioning system for another couple of weeks. It had to be flown in from Germany or somewhere.

'Unacceptable. These conditions are inhumane,' wrote Daniel.

And in the end, something must have worked because the temperature went up, the administrative team kept their jobs, the company did not move to new, warmer premises and Daniel began to work again.

And this is when I came in.

'Just be yourself,' said Helena. 'You're good at your job. Now let's see you apply it.' And she sent me in there.

At our first meeting I was overwhelmed by him for a little while. In his presence, I felt the stirring of the gift again, and pushed it down, trying to ignore it. Daniel was tall, and had the watery-red eyes of a man who sat in front of a computer until five each morning, designing and building software. All I knew about him was rumour. I had heard he hated women. I had heard all the stories about how he'd had people fired. I had heard he'd said in public that if anybody tried to change his documents, or re-write them in any way, he'd get them sacked, and then he'd think about leaving the company himself, the latter being the bigger threat.

Five minutes into the meeting, he made a pun that was so bad I forgot it as soon as I stopped laughing. And then he asked a question about fonts and I looked at him carefully and saw that I had nothing to fear from this man's intellect. I had more to fear from his loneliness and hurting heart, the way he used withdrawal as defence, his solitude enforced by fear. I looked at him and saw that this was where our problems would lie, because I ached to reach out to touch him, to make it better. Fonts would be a pushover compared with all that other stuff.

The font question turned out to be a test that I inadvertently passed with a serendipitous combination of caution and knowledge.

'What do you feel about the fact that we use a sans serif font for the body text in our documents here?' he asked.

'Well,' I replied carefully, 'I was originally taught that you should use a serif font for blocks of text and a sans serif font for headings — that it's easier to understand the contents of a document that way.' And then I said, by way of prevarication, 'But opinions on this often differ, you know, and I've heard people say that for every paper proving that this is true, there is another that says different.'

It was the perfect opening for him. 'Aha,' he said. 'I'm glad you said that, because I read recently, in a scientific journal to which I subscribe ...' (and yes, he really spoke like that in antiquated, well-thought-out grammar, with structure weighted heavily towards what your first grade teacher managed to teach you with the aid of a metre-long wooden ruler that she did not hesitate to use when the need arose) 'that the serif aids cognition and comprehension.'

'Oh really?' and I felt my eyebrows raise in what I hoped was an expression of mild surprise. 'I've also heard though,' I said, 'that the effectiveness of any font depends, to a certain extent, on the relationship between its size, the space between the lines of text and the line length, so it is difficult to make judgements about particular typefaces without seeing them in context. So, I suppose you could say,' I continued, 'that there is no research that says that either serif or sans serif fonts are intrinsically more legible.'

He smiled at me across the desk. I could not recall anybody ever telling me he smiled.

'Let's take a look at these documents,' he said.

PROSPECT

The Princess calls weekly with updates on her new man. She is in love again, or so she suspects, with Robert, who thankfully is turning out to be very good to her. He is a patient man. She has started spending weekends at his house and they are, you believe, dating exclusively. Apparently she is not playing the field any more, and that in itself has significance for the Princess, a woman who says that she is 'single until she is engaged'. And meanwhile, having lost a drinking companion to the adventures of the heart, you at least have your books as a substitute for conversations you used to have with her. And you are still alone. Perhaps you need to have a house-warming, since you have been here for some time now and not done that yet. It is probably time to have a dinner party.

You decide to put Aubrey on the list of people you will invite, even though he has not tried to call again. You call the Princess. She is excited.

'Oooh Theney! A dinner party! Let me help!'

'Okay. Invite a couple of people. I only know a few, and only about three I want to invite to dinner.'

'Absolutely. I'll think of someone nice.'

As you go ahead with the arrangements, something feels odd. You can't put your finger on it and there is no reason to feel the way you do. In the end, you shrug the oddness off and just get on with your plans. Closer to the day you realise — it is him you want to see. You want to see Aubrey. You have called and left a message inviting him to the dinner. He has not called back. You call again. He answers and his voice is tired.

'I'm having a bad time ... I'm going through some stuff. I really don't think ...'

'Well, you know the date, you know my address ...'

He sighs. 'I'll try. I'll try real hard. But I can't guarantee anything. And if I can make it I'll probably be late.'

'Dinner with an angel? You'd turn that down?'

'That wasn't a joke, Theney,' he says sharply. 'I wasn't kidding around when I told you about that.' He pauses. You've hurt him. He thinks you were laughing at him. 'I probably won't come.'

But you are starting to feel a bubble — a golden bubble in your heart expanding slowly and sweetly. You are allowing it to grow a little, but you're scared at the same time that something will prick it and burst it.

You shop for the party with secret smiles, choosing the things you know how to cook well; things to bake and stew, the ingredients for bread, and beautiful desserts. You want to fill your house with smells that will give you back your mother. Besides, you have heard that the way to a man's heart is through his stomach, and you know you are good at stomachs. In the quiet moments as you cook for him, as you mix things and bake them, test them for done-ness in the oven, taste them to be sure you have your combinations right, you let yourself think that maybe this Aubrey is going to be something special. It seems like such a long time since you were just held and looked at with liquid eyes ... and isn't it true that life without love is a sad and dreary life and not altogether healthy? Hadn't you been a good girl and earned some love? Isn't that how it works? Good girl equals loved girl?

You had forgotten for a moment that algebra is not a life science.

DOTTIE'S NOTEBOOK

A life has many starts and stops and something stopped and started with Daniel.

'I trust you,' he said, after working with me for two weeks.

I made no changes to his documents without his permission. He agreed with all my proposed changes. And I began, despite myself, to enjoy his company and let myself relax.

'No woman's treated me this well, for more years than I care to remember,' he said one day.

'I'm not a woman, I'm a technical writer,' I quipped. And I saw his mood change instantly and realised that something had begun.

I had never touched him, never done that thing that seemed to cause havoc whenever I let it take me over. I was getting good at avoiding taking action, but with Daniel I knew I had to do something. It was too hard to resist with him. If he had been blind I would have done what I could to assist, or if he'd been deaf, or missing a limb. For me, with him, there was no difference between these ailments and his particular brand of suffering.

We had lunch together most days. I spent days in his office, working on his documents. He arranged to have my computer moved in there so we could work together. The documents I created with him were a great success — people loved them. Sales figures improved because the documentation clearly showed the features and benefits of the product. Support calls reduced because people found the manuals easy to read. But my colleagues began to be nervous around me. They looked at me as though I had done something wrong. Part of me agreed and felt strangely guilty for the way he had taken to me, and I to him. I was junior and new to this game. I had no business succeeding where others had failed.

But I *had* succeeded and so, when the company decided to create a website, and I found out that the web team needed a writer, or more precisely a 'content developer', I asked Daniel whether he thought I should apply.

'I can write HTML,' I said, having just learned what it stood for, but not actually having figured out how it worked yet. I knew I was up to the challenge, and I was desperate to escape the judgement of my colleagues. A new team, away from them, and the excitement of learning Hypertext Markup Language before anyone discovered my ignorance would be just what I needed.

'Okay,' said Daniel, who had the ear of the website project manager (he had the ear of anyone he cared to). He knew I knew nothing, I found out later, but wanted to see what happened if he got me the job. And so I became the content manager for the company's brand new intranet, extranet and knowledge management system.

After work, when I needed somewhere to go, Lolita's Flamenco Bar was my place. At least, it seemed reasonable to think of it as mine — I found myself there at least twice a week and I was addicted (just a little) to that passion-music, the way it vibrated in that little space at the base of my throat, where the passion lives. I would sit and watch, entranced, and if I had consumed enough Bulls' Blood wine, would dance and clap and feel a female energy running across the floor from the stomping feet of the flamenco dancers right to my chair, and up my legs, and pausing just a second in my womb to vibrate and then up my stomach and between my breasts and right into that secret place to drive me wild with what it feels like to be female and fertile and desperately missing having a man in my bed.

And, though he was wombless, when Daniel began to join me at Lolita's regularly, he enjoyed it too. I suppose I was falling for him so I turned it, in a strange way, into something the two of us had in common instead of just … much less. A lanky streak of clouded misery was how the rest of the world saw him, but I began to see him shine. A silver light that was barely present when we first met began to surround him more. As it grew, it seemed to guard him. I began to feel that with just another deeper glance, another tiny measurement of depth that was not millimetres or time or any sort of measurement I'd ever been able to name or explain but have simply known about all my life, I could have connected with him completely.

And then I took a risk and it all went wrong. I offered him a lift back to his apartment after Melbourne Cup lunch. I had my car, and he was drunk. I made it sound as though I was going in his direction already, though I wasn't. It seemed important somehow, to hide from him that I just wanted him in my car, so I could sit next to him and tell him all the things that were in my heart, knowing what I knew about the way he felt as well, though he had never said a word. How was I to know that a person can feel something and refuse, refuse to look at it. Or be unable to. But whether they won't or they can't the end result is the same.

I was driving up High Street and mostly I remember sun on my arm, which I had out the window out of habit; and sun through the windscreen on the black interior of the car, which was over twenty years old and beige and terrible for my image as a person in control of her own destiny. I kept it going mainly by topping up the oil and water whenever I stopped for petrol and by patting it on the dashboard when it needed encouragement. I praised it when it started on cold mornings and babied it through peak hour traffic on the way home at five-thirty in the afternoon. It had that perished vinyl smell that old cars have, and whenever I think of that horrible moment with Daniel, I smell it. To this day, I swear I could never buy a car that smells like that again.

And anyway, we were on High Street, about to turn left down Glenferrie Road, and there was a music store to our right and behind us and suddenly the staff in the store decided to play some romantic love song sung by some crooner over the outside speakers. I could not look at Daniel, sitting there beside me. The tension was awful and, just before the traffic lights turned green, I said — Heaven help me, I actually said — 'You know how I feel about you, don't you?'

Heh. No response. But now I had started I could not stop, and if I had asked anybody they would have said that that was probably not the best time to be in control of a car, mainly because I would have been out of control, which I was. I told him he was all I dreamed of and how I knew he'd never talked to me about it, but I thought perhaps he felt the same, and that I needed to tell him how I felt because the way things were was eating away at me. I told him too much. I have a memory of passing a tram too fast and being in the wrong gear, running away from my own words, but I was in the car with them and with him and I really couldn't stop telling him that he was everything to me, and at the same time I also knew inside what a fool I was being and probably throwing away the friendship that I had with him. Not to mention work. How would I ever be able to look at him again?

And he said: 'I thought we were friends.'

Special spectacles, if I'd had them, would have shown my words strewn around the car, spewed up from the place where I had been hiding all those feelings for all that time. Why is it that passion felt alone can be as strong and difficult as razors? Does the passion of another for you soften it somehow and take away the edges?

In the debris I sat and said, 'I'm sorry ... I shouldn't

have …' But it was too late. Even before I started speaking I had known I shouldn't have, but that sensible option had been buried under the terrible need to spill my guts. And then it was too late and all the words were laid out. So I sat there in the hot November sun in a car that smelled like perished vinyl and I felt like a lump, a hot and sweaty worthless lump — not lovable — not anything, but sick to the stomach and maybe minus one friend.

He got out of the car and went inside his building and when I saw him at work the next day, I realised he had found a way to forgive me, though I would never forgive myself for my stupidity. He still came out to Lolita's and sat with me, and I thought this was the best way. For a long time afterwards my feelings for him remained strong, and I hoped that either he would turn to me one day and admit that he loved me, or that I would wake up one morning and not want that any more. And then one night at Lolita's bar, eating tapas, drinking beer, waiting for the music to start, I watched the light around him and I knew that tonight something was different. I felt that little knowledge knot that happens when I know something to be true with my heart and stomach before my head has figured it out.

He said 'I've got a friend coming down from Sydney. She's meeting me here.'

'He has friends, in Sydney? How did that happen?' was the only thought I had behind the 'Mmm, that's nice' I uttered, tinged with nervousness.

Then she walked in the door and his light was all a-flutter. A silent wail behind my throat began the moment I saw him look at her. A cry, like ululation to the unfair sky: *'She's his, he can't even see me'*. Then, the wailing question in my mind — to which I already knew the answer — *'My God, what's wrong with me?'*

PROSPECT

You put the Princess in charge of champagne. And since Robert is also there, she delegates to him, all smiles and coquetry.

'Honey, can you open this for me?'

When you are at her house the job is yours. You wonder what she does when she drinks champagne all alone. Perhaps she never has to drink champagne all alone.

People trickle in and soon there are seven of you. You decide to start without him. Dinner, what a dinner; with the light just so, all yellow and warm, over a large table full of people eating your food, listening to your music, laughing. Your mother always told you that the true sign of a good dinner party is when the table has a flow, a rhythm of its own and you can walk away without being missed. And this is how it is: at one end a conversation all seriousness, intent on discovering some new truth that is destined to be lost later in the folds of a thumping hangover. And up here at the other end, a competition of sorts for who could tell the silliest joke, and before anything becomes set, it has moved again, and that table and its food and its people and its bottles and all its self has come to life and had that warmth in it, that mix of past and future that makes it somehow a symbol of hope.

It is an hour or so into the dinner before you accept that Aubrey isn't coming. He doesn't answer when you phone him. You do not leave a message, but if he has caller ID on his phone, he will see that you rang. You hope he doesn't have caller ID.

Robert and the Princess sit together, at one end of the table. Something about it reminds you of the night that you went out with Daniel and his new girlfriend, the one who made his light flutter. The three of you went out to a club in St Kilda, where the tonic water in Daniel's drink glowed iridescent in the lights behind the bar downstairs. Country girl that you were, you had never seen anything like it. There were three rooms in the club and a different band in each. The three of you moved from room to room, dancing and talking, until you gave up and left them to each other. As you left the club, the sun was greying the sky, and the newness of it cheered you up a little. You could picture them the next morning, golden skinned, sprawled on the bed in Daniel's house, naked and belonging to each other. You didn't see it, nor did they ever talk about it, but you knew; you had known what it was before it came true.

And now in Prospect, Nebraska, your dinner table seems to be full of couples. You top up your wine and look across at the Princess and Robert. There is a tension between them you want to dissipate. It has to be right for them. They have to become a good couple. He has to take away the anxiety that makes her sabotage her own happiness. She has to love him in a way that makes him feel safe. You silently will them to be happy. They must. What hope would there be for you if they are not?

The evening draws to a close, and the warm murmurs turn to smiling goodbyes and the sound of boots crunching away from you on the snow. They leave, two by two, and you are left alone, with the debris. There's dessert left, and a glassful of wine in the bottom of a bottle, so you indulge, but end up moving apple crumble from side to side on your plate and ruining it with salty tears.

DOTTIE'S NOTEBOOK

In that dark time, as I learned to cope with unrequited love, there was another blow.

Dottie used to call me every month or so from San Antonio. She made sure we stayed close. She used to tell me 'I just want to see how my Theney's going.' She was my angel. When the phone rang on that Sunday, I knew I didn't want to pick it up. And I knew it was Dottie.

'What's wrong?' I asked, even before I said hello.

Dottie had a smile in her voice. 'Ahh, Theney, I should have guessed you would feel it.'

'Dottie, what's happened?'

'I'm dying, pet.'

The grief that hit me was a physical thing. It floored me. 'Dottie, no.'

'Yes, my love. It's true. And it's all right. I am in no pain. I know it will be easy.'

'What happened?'

'Well, I had a stroke, and we're all expecting me to have more. I'm paralysed down one side. Actually, I'm in the hospital now. They keep telling me lies about how I'm going to get better. But you remember how I told

100

you I have some of Grandma Dot's gift? Theney, I know I'm going. It's the end of my visit here and I feel perfectly fine about that. I've had a wonderful time.'

'I'll come over. I can leave today.' I was already calculating bank balances and time zones.

'No pet, you don't have to. Remember me alive, love. Don't fill your head with images of me paralysed and dying.'

'Is there anything I can do? I want to do something … I want to take your pain away.'

'I am in no pain, pet.'

I knew she was lying. She knew I knew. My heart broke a little.

'I love you, Theney.'

'Oh, Dottie. I love you too. I am going to miss you more than I can bear. What will I do?'

'Now, pet, you'll be all right. Blessings on your head, my love.'

And that was it.

A few weeks later a solicitor in Johnson Street — two doors down from Lolita's Flamenco Bar — sent me a letter requesting a meeting because he had news that concerned me and the estate of Ms Doris Frances Abercrombie, recently deceased while resident in San Antonio, Texas. I had never known that Dottie and I shared the same middle name.

PROSPECT

When the phone wakes you at three a.m. you reach across the empty pillow beside you and pick it up without thinking, expecting it will be the Princess; expecting that the tension you saw at the dinner table has turned into something more verbal or worse and she and Robert have split, with angry words and misunderstandings.

Instead, it is Aubrey's voice that says, hesitantly, 'Did I wake you?'

'No … Yes. Mmm I was only halfway there,' you say.

'How was your dinner party?' he says.

'Good. Good. I missed you.' It slipped out because you were tired, and you had no way of stopping it.

Silence at his end. 'I'm sorry. I had to do a gig. A last minute thing. Birthday party.'

'Oh.'

'I just got home.'

You are silent.

'I see that you called.'

So he has caller ID. You say 'Yes. Yes, I did. Sorry.' Shit. Why do Australians always do that? Sorry for what?

For wanting him to come to the dinner party and for calling to see why he wasn't there? You struggle to wake.

'I should have called you, let you know.'

'Maybe. But you didn't.'

'No. I'm a shit.'

'Maybe. I hope not.'

'Can I see you?'

'Now?'

'Yes ... Well, maybe not. Bad idea. I just want to talk.'

'What about?'

'Things I can't talk about on the phone.'

'Okay.'

'Okay what?'

'Okay you can see me. Okay you can see me right now. I'm awake now, you might as well come over.' What are you *saying*? Shut up shut up shut up shut up.

'Great,' he says. 'Give me your address again. I've lost the piece of paper I wrote it on.'

When he knocks on your door, you are sitting on the stairs waiting. You open the door to him. He takes off his coat and boots.

'Nice suit,' you say.

'It was one of those gigs,' he says.

You take his hand and lead him up the stairs. 'If you want to talk to me, you have to do it up here. I'm tired. I need to lie down.'

'Okay. Can I have a glass of water?'

'You can share mine.'

You lie down on your side of the bed, draw the covers up to your chin.

103

He stands beside the other side, confused. 'I just wanted to talk. I don't want to, you know, do anything …'

'I know. Me neither. Just get in. Tell me what you have to tell me.'

You turn off the light and from the corner of your eye, in the moonlight, you see him taking off his pants, jacket and socks.

The bed moves as he gets in. 'Oh, it's warm!' he says.

'I turned the blanket on after you rang,' you say. 'Now, what did you want to tell me.'

'Let's just lie here for a minute,' he says. 'This is nice.' You turn to face him and as your eyes adjust, you see that he is turned to look at you, with a little smile. 'You're an odd one, Theney,' he says.

'You have no idea what truth you speak.'

He reaches out his hand and touches your hair. You turn your face to kiss the palm of his hand, then bring your own hand out from under the covers and interlace your fingers with his and it is like this that the two of you fall quietly asleep, with no further words spoken.

Some hours later, you wake in his arms. He has them around you, and his body curled around yours. You can hear his quiet breathing. In the morning, he's gone. No note, no message. Just an indent in the pillow and a quarter and a nickel on the carpet on his side of the bed, fallen, you presume, out of one of his pant pockets.

I went to Helena and told her I had to go. I handed her the letter of resignation that I had read and re-read before coming into her office. 'I'm resigning.'

Helena motioned me into one of her visitors' chairs, and came around the desk to sit beside me. She took my hand. 'I understand,' she said. 'Dot was a dear friend to me for many years. And for you, it's worse. Your aunt has died, you've had some things going on. I really do understand.' I seemed to hear her through a fog. But then, that's how everything felt in those dark days.

She leaned towards me. 'We don't want to lose you. I thought you might do this and I have an idea. Would you be prepared to stop in our offices in Nebraska and do some work for us there? They're good people, and they need someone like you for a couple of months.'

I looked at her. 'I don't need to work any more,' I said. 'Dottie left me a lot of money and a house in America. It's in San Antonio, Texas. I don't even know where Nebraska is. I only just found Texas on a map.'

'I know, I know,' she said. 'But just think about it. No strings, two months of work you'd probably enjoy — and you'd really be helping us out.'

The last bit was the clincher. 'Okay,' I said.

On the way from Melbourne to San Antonio, via Los Angeles, I stopped for the promised 'maximum two months' of work for the company's office in Prospect, Nebraska where now, after a year, I am still stopped. In the midst of snow and unfamiliar faces, I cling to little events and accidents thinking they are part of a pattern or a plan or a purpose — but perhaps there is no purpose. Perhaps Dottie was right and I just need to live in this moment and remember it well when it is passed and honour it with truth, and that will be enough.

A month after I arrived, they asked me to stay for a year. They like me here. And I have to admit, I like the feeling of being somewhere new, where nobody knows who I was or anything about me, except what I choose to tell them. 'Get our intranet in line with the one in the Melbourne office,' they said. 'A new design, better content, a global presence,' they said. 'We could really use your skills,' they said. The Melbourne office said it was okay, and Terry, my new boss in the Prospect office, was excited when I agreed to give it a go.

'It's so great to have someone from the Australian office here,' he said. 'You can really do some good work.'

'I'm supposed to be in San Antonio,' I said. 'Dealing with some family things.'

'You can always fly to San Antonio,' he said. 'It's not far. Take some leave any time you need to. But stay with us awhile. You'll love it here in Prospect, we know. It's a great place to live.'

And then, under the impression that if I could create a perfect environment to live in it would be the key to happiness, I decided that if I were going to stay in Prospect I should move out of the company apartment and find a place that was mine, by myself. I imagined some bohemian place with wooden panels and books and music and an interesting untidiness. Imagined people in it, too, and maybe just around the corner there might be someone I could take home and love and be loved by — although I imagined I would always wish it could be Daniel.

I started my search downtown, which is where the cool apartments are — the hip and interesting places, with the seedy feel imparted by the age and decrepitude of the buildings, the dirty windows with the bedraggled houseplants, yellow from the lack of water or the oversupply of coffee or tea or bong water. Or too much cigarette and other ash tapped into them by what I imagined to be a reclining corduroy-wearing intelligentsia, or bohemian artist sets, spouting forth, over red wine and coffee, about the things that I wished I could also spout forth about. I hadn't found my niche in the world and it felt like it was time for that to happen.

So guided, as I sometimes think I am, I clumsily walked in heels too high (it was my first winter and I hadn't taken the icy footpaths into account when choosing what to wear) across the ice to the hippest, coolest apartment block in town, which was a converted grainstore. I had made an appointment with some building manager's nasal voice and I buzzed and buzzed but there was no answer at the door. A passing thought that maybe this was a sign that I should heed, and I left, disappointed, and went to find somewhere to have a cup of coffee and a think about what to do next.

PROSPECT

Breakfast in America is one of your favourite things, and you have found your favourite places to enjoy it. If you want to feel like you just stepped into a movie from fifty years ago, you go to the diner downtown that looks like a shack. In fact, you seem to end up there every Saturday morning lately. With studded crimson vinyl seats, the booths have music selectors — choose a song from one of the metal pages hanging there, put your quarter in, press the numbers and then the jukebox starts to play. There's one booth where you can feed quarters into the slot and punch numbers until the cows come home and no music ever comes out. You tried, the first time, to retrieve your money, but then the waitress standing beside you turned towards the kitchen and yelled 'Jerry!' and he yelled 'Yeah?' from where he stood flipping breakfast sausages and eggs.

'Is this the one that's broke?' she yelled.

'Sure is,' he yelled back. 'And there ain't no way we can get the money out, no-how, darn-fool thing's jammed.'

And she shrugged her shoulders at you then filled up

your coffee, and later brought two quarters to you from the till with a wink.

This diner is the one you choose this Saturday, as usual, for your coffee and whatever breakfast takes your fancy from the battered laminated menu or the list of specials on the blackboard by the door. The sign is still up in the window, advertising for casual staff. It's been there for weeks. There don't seem to be any new people here. Just the same old faces. Maybe you could get a job here. It could be an adventure.

The door opens with a blast of cold air, and somebody walks in to the diner. It's Aubrey. You move the menu right in front of you and surreptitiously lower yourself in your seat. You've never seen him in here before.

'Hi.' He's walking your way. 'Hi,' he says. 'Mind if I join you?' He sits. 'May I?' He reaches across the table for the menu you have just laid down. He studies it, his finger on his lip, considering.

This is the first time that you've actually managed to take a look at him, properly, in daylight. You can still see the light around him. It is like no light you have seen around a person before, even Daniel, and you wonder what that means. It draws you, that is certain. Something seems to be throwing him in your path. You have come to believe in these things — that people pop up for a reason, that very little happens by accident.

The reasons themselves usually escape you, but you have faith that they exist. In flippant conversations in the past, you have said that if you cannot believe that life makes sense, then you might as well just jump off a cliff. The thought of a life's struggle with no purpose is terrifying.

You continue to look at him. He has dark reddish-brown hair, with salt and pepper creeping in. Deep eyes, an Irish look about their liquid-dark-blueness. A high forehead. When he stands he is close to two metres tall, but sitting down, you see he has a tendency to hunch. His hands are large, strong and clean. You remember that from when you first met. He looks up and catches you studying him.

'What do you see?'

'A puzzle.'

'How so?'

'Do you believe in fate?'

He snorts. 'That's a ridiculous question.'

'Why?'

'For one thing, it's too big to deal with before I've had a coffee.' Pam the waitress materialises and he orders. 'Coffee (extra cream), two eggs (over easy), hash browns, sausages (links), toast (white).'

Pam looks at you.

'Eggs Benedict. Hollandaise on the side.' You point to your cup. 'And a refill.'

'Sure honey. Be right back.'

He leans back. 'Do you believe in angels?'

'This again? Do you believe in love?'

'Romantic love? Romantic love is an ideologically suspect construct.'

'Oh please. How old are you? Forty-five?'

'Why? Does it matter?'

'If you are male and single and you're forty-five or

over you automatically have old man's disease. Men get to a certain age and if they're not with a partner it's because they've been terribly betrayed. More betrayed than anyone could possibly understand, and they deal with it by making bitter pronouncements like that one.'

'How old are you?'

'Why? Does it matter?' You smile at him, surprised at how much fun you are having.

'I'm guessing you're in your early thirties. Women your age always think they have the right to give advice to anyone who'll stop long enough to listen.'

'Ouch.'

'Let's get back to my original question,' he said. 'Do you believe in angels?'

'Can you make the question easier to understand?'

He's exasperated. 'How much clearer ...? Look, will you come with me after breakfast? I'd really like to show you something.'

'I might have somewhere to go,' you say, leaning forward.

'It's Saturday. And I know you don't work weekends. Shopping can wait. The malls are open tomorrow.'

'You can trust me,' he goes on. 'I'm a jazz musician.'

'Let me think.'

'Don't think. Just do it. You need to do it.'

'You're making it impossible to say no.'

'Yup.'

'Is it an outside or an inside thing?'

'Outside. Sanderson Forest.'

'We have to go in your car. I have to leave a note with the Princess. I need to get a warmer coat.'

'I'm flattered you trust me.'

'I don't,' you laugh. 'But I'll take the risk. Any cousin of Lloyd's ... And besides, it's broad daylight and I'm from wilder places than this. You've got no idea what you're dealing with.' You realise as you say it that your blustering bravado has not come out the way you meant it to. But he lets it go with not even a raised eyebrow.

DOTTIE'S NOTEBOOK

I had been disconcerted by the absence of any cafés in Prospect like the ones I used to frequent in Melbourne. Here, in the chain coffee stores they have in the two enormous chain bookstores I had discovered in the malls in the suburbs, I had found out that I had to choose my coffee from a bewildering menu full of unfamiliar combinations of milk, flavouring and size. The concept of two percent milk bothered me at first. I wondered what the other ninety-eight percent was. And then I found out it referred to fat content and wondered why not just call it skim? What would at home have been a simple question of asking for a long black or a flat white resulted here in an initial shocked stiffening and wide eyes, or a glazed 'Huh?' or an embarrassing combination of them both as I messed with all sorts of political incorrectness by asking for coffee by colour. And I had always thought the warnings they had given me at the office about the "crap coffee" were just a joke, an exaggeration by those who had travelled here and now used their superior knowledge to show off to other less travelled unfortunates. It only took me a few weeks to realise that their warnings were no joke.

I stood at the counter and looked at the board on the back wall, trying to figure out which coffee on the list came closest to what I wanted. But I gave up. 'Peppermint tea, please,' I said to the gum-chewing teenager behind the counter, and then for no good reason, 'What's the best way to look for an apartment in Prospect?'

'I have no idea, really,' she said brightly. 'I guess you could look in the paper, though.'

A voice beside me said, 'Excuse me, I couldn't help but overhear. I might be able to help.'

I turned and saw a woman with a friendly smile. 'Hi,' she said. She held out her hand and introduced herself. Soon afterwards, when I came to know her better, I named her the Princess. Her real name is one of those American ones that I had previously assumed had been invented for daytime television or sitcoms, until I actually came to this country and realised that there are real people walking around called Brooke and Stacy and Shelley and Laurie and Courtney. And not just a few. They were everywhere I looked, and they were blonde and Barbie-plastic, or aspiring to be. Although I acknowledge that I do have a tendency to use a broad judgmental brush when it would be the mark of a better person if I were to look for the positive, to note instead the gifts that each of these individuals could offer. But somehow, it just never happens like that.

Later, when the two of us became friends, we found out that we both believed that some things are meant to be — and that is how meeting the Princess feels even a year later. She said she was looking at a newly refurbished apartment block not far from there and she was going to check out the apartments as soon as she'd finished her coffee. She said they were converted warehouses.

'I've heard they're really interesting,' she said. 'Quite unusual. I like to live in interesting places.' She hesitated a moment then asked, 'Would you care to come with?', with that strange Mid-Western way of dropping the pronoun off the end.

I was even more of a believer in signs and messages then than I am now and I thought this had to qualify as either one or the other. I smiled and thanked her and joined her at a small table where we drank our coffee and tea and made small talk.

Outside, she showed me her car. 'Just follow me,' she said. 'It's five minutes from here.'

The apartment was gloriously right and all I had been hoping for. It had everything, and I was enchanted by who I might become by renting it. I could really re-invent myself there, fill it with books and furniture that inspired me. I could make a little place for me to nestle in. And fill it with new friends that I was sure I would soon be making; fill it with laughter and wine and freshly baked bread.

A week later I was signing a lease for the newly painted freshness of it, for the white walls, terracotta tiles, and ceilings high and white. It felt like I was signing a lease for more than an apartment. I filled the house with furniture and scented candles. I bought bookcases and began to fill them with books. I filled the fridge with food. It felt as though I had found my home.

PROSPECT

'Come,' says Aubrey, parking the car in the virtually de-
serted carpark. 'It's just a little ways up ahead. We have
to go through here first.'

He opens the door of the visitors' centre and you walk
into a room that has the musty smell and all the dusty
decorations of a museum. Before the two of you can
walk in the wilderness you need to pay three dollars at
the desk which extends into the gift shop. The proof
that three dollars has been handed over is a sticker that
is to be worn at all times while in the forest. *'Or what?'*
you think to yourself. *'Or bloody what?'* It smacks of the
same unthinking acquiescence to authority that has surprised you more than once here when you have watched
civilian people talk to military people. Something so different to the automatic suspicion that has somehow
leaked into the Australian psyche, the unspoken assump-
tion that authority is to be questioned; is to be reminded
constantly that it has to earn respect, and cannot automatically expect it with the donning of a uniform. So
you put your sticker in your jacket pocket, instead of on
the lapel, and notice that Aubrey watches you and does

the same. Seeds of dissent. Ned Kelly would have been proud.

Past the counter where the fee is paid there is a room, and on its walls are cages and boxes containing stuffed animals in reconstructed habitat. Birds and forest creatures that you might see on the trails. In the centre of the room is a glass covered box and in it lies a snake, coiled and miserable. Well, it's hard to tell its mood, but how could it be happy in that box, with the glass eyes of the dead staring at it through the day and night? You wonder what it would normally do at this time of year, with the ground frozen and all the little mice and other prey gone into hiding for the winter.

Aubrey lets you walk through the room slowly, taking in the details of this ante-room to the forest. But then you reach the metal doors that open out onto a wooden deck.

'So where's the wilderness?' you ask.

'We have to get away from the building a ways,' he says. 'It isn't far, perhaps a mile.'

In front of you the wooden platform forks and becomes two boardwalks, which divide again a little way ahead, a network of wooden paths above the twigs, leaf-mould and snow. In front of you a map in sixteen different colours names the different routes through the forest. Beside you, to the right, there is an owl in a cage whose placard says it was rescued and cannot fly and never will, and is cared for by the staff and is, they say, a kind of mascot.

Walking over, you say 'Hello' and hook your fingers into the wire of the cage before you see the sign that tells you not to do this. His beak, says the sign, is very strong. The owl stares at you unblinkingly and yellow-eyed and has the softest feathers on its neck. It reminds you unexpectedly of nights when you were just a girl, camping out beneath Bald Hill, where you would some-times go to watch the sunrise. The boobook owl would call at night and its soft hooting would make you feel that all was well. Looking at the short neck and the round feathered face you can suddenly see and smell the Grey box trees and stringybarks, hear the cockatoos that nested in the branches near the creek, feel the anticipa-tion of tomorrow's brand new rays as they topped the hill to catch you by surprise with their beauty, no matter how many times you saw them. Some nights, the bush could be too big and you heard a menace in its quiet nighttime noises. But the boobook was a soothing sound and the best nights were the ones where you could see it silhouetted on a branch or swooping past, intent on bogong moths or native mice.

You grip the cage and put your face against the cold steel wire and the owl continues to look at you. It could be stuffed, it sits so still, but then it blinks. A slow delib-erate lidding and unlidding that speaks louder than speech.

'Hail Friend', you think and let Aubrey call you away.

'What's up?' he says.

'I had to say hello.'

'You're a bit strange.'

'I warned you. You have no idea.' You follow him into the forest, looking backwards only once.

The boardwalk forms an easy walking loop around the

visitors' centre and at its furthest point steps lead down and onto a dirt path. A sign with an arrow points to Milson's Ridge.

'That's where we're headed,' he points.

'Lead on,' you say, and follow his back into the trees. He's cutting a fast pace and soon you have your jacket off and tied around your waist, as he does. The gloves stay on, but the freezing air feels good on your neck and freshens you even through the long-johns and the flannel shirt.

He turns. 'You doing okay?'

A smile. 'Yes, thanks. Can't wait to see where you're taking me.'

'Maybe,' he says, 'just maybe, it'll answer all your questions.' But he's just being funny, you're sure.

'I mightn't have any questions.'

'You talk to owls — you have questions.'

Something on the path catches your eye. It is a feather, about thirty centimetres long, with distinctive brown and white stripes all along its length. You've seen feathers like it, but half a world away. It is an owl feather, you would almost bet money on it — you've seen so many like them on a different forest floor. You had one, just like it, on your dressing table for years. It's from a tail or wing, strong, and without the slightest imperfection.

'Look!' you say, and Aubrey turns and you hold it out to him. 'It's a feather,' you explain, 'an owl feather! Here, you take it.'

'Who are you?' he asks, reaching for it, 'Athena?' He laughs.

'That's my name,' you laugh back. 'That's what Theney's short for.'

'That was dumb of me,' he says. 'I should have guessed. You *are* Athena!'

'Don't you have those types of days,' you ask, 'when it's as though someone is trying to tell you something?'

'Yes,' he says, 'but it's usually about how I should stop drinking or whoring. Can we keep on, please?'

You stop short. 'What?'

Instead of answering he turns and steps away, still holding the feather. You hurry to catch up, and see a flitting shape above him in the trees. It couldn't be, but it is.

'Aubrey! An owl!' You point.

He shades his eyes and looks up. 'Where? Can't see anything.'

'Up there, to the right. Follow my finger.'

'Can't see it. Let's get going. If you need a rest, you should just say so. Do you need a rest?'

'No.' You're still looking up.

'Come on.'

He moves ahead and you follow, watching the scraps of sky above you to see the shape again. It reappears and flies from tree to tree, just ahead of you. You could imagine it as a guide or a protector, though it may just be on its own path, unrelated to your own.

The path begins to climb steeply to the ridge and soon you are concentrating on following Aubrey, his khaki shirt hanging out, a little sweat-stain between the shoulder blades. It is a strong back. You could get to like it. The thing about the owls is playing with your mind a little. A sudden sense of destiny washes through you, but you shake it off. The trees thin and the two of you emerge onto a high grass plain. You haven't seen a soul since you arrived. Incongruous, a park bench on a concrete plinth is just ahead. Aubrey walks towards it.

'We're here,' he says

You rest a moment on the bench together, happy to be silent and tired. After a while he touches your shoulder to get your attention and points ahead. There, amongst the conifers and leafless winter trees, stands an anomaly. Surrounded by the deep green and lifeless greys of the other trees stands a golden tree so bright it seems to glow from within.

'What is that, do you think?' he asks

'Don't know. I don't know my North American trees very well.' You pause. 'It is beautiful, though.'

'Oh,' he says. 'So you think it's a tree?'

'What else would it be? I see leaves, I see a trunk. Of course it's …'

'Bit late in the season for fall colours, don't you think?'

'Some trees are late. A pinoak keeps its leaves on all winter, even though they're dead.'

'But what colour are the pinoak leaves?'

'Brown … admittedly.'

'I think perhaps, it's an angel … perhaps an angel.'

You almost laugh, but look across first to see if he is serious. 'You're serious.'

'Why not? An angel is just a physical manifestation of psychic energy. You think they've all got wings and robes and harps?'

'No, but …'

'Well there you are then. I look at that vision before us, with its golden shimmering cloak, and I know it's not just a tree — nothing that glows like that could be just a tree.'

'What's it doing out here?'

'Well, what about your freaking owls then? How do you explain that?'

'I'm not calling them angels.'

He reaches across and puts the feather in your woollen hat. 'Here, but don't let the ranger see you with it. They've got rules about taking things out of the forest.' And then he reaches out to hold your hand and bends his head towards you and kisses you, something that doesn't surprise you. What surprises you is that you allow it and enjoy it.

It only lasts a minute, then you rest; but now he has his arm across the back of the bench and you are nestled into him, with your hand under his thigh, the weight of his strong leg comforting you somehow.

'It's been like this all winter. I've never noticed it in other years,' he says.

'Have you been up close, to take a look?' you ask. 'Perhaps there is a rational explanation.'

'It's not about knowledge. A rational explanation would destroy it. This way I can believe what I want, and it's true.'

He puts his hand on your neck, touches the secret place there, beneath your hair.

'So is that what you believe, that it's an angel?' you ask.

'Theney.' The gentleness in his voice is uncomfortable

and demands that you be flippant in response. Flippancy is always a good way to avoid danger.

'Did you know that the goddess Athena jumped out of her father's head instead of being born the usual way?' You sit up and take the feather out of your cap, turning away from him to wedge it into a crack at the back of the seat.

'Yes,' he laughs. 'But I'm not sure that's how she's best remembered. She's the goddess of battles, a warrior goddess.'

'Goddess of War,' you say.

'No,' he says. 'Not war. It's important to be precise. War is a destructive phenomenon. Battles, and the need for warrior spirit, well, they'll be with us as long as we are human. She was a warrior goddess, and the goddess of battles, and when she manifested in the human world, it was to protect and guide heroes. And the battles that we fight on this earth, in the here and now, are also her realm. And she is the goddess of wisdom as well. You know, owls and such. She was not destructive of things for destruction's sake. Though Medusa might not agree. Did you know that Medusa was a beautiful woman who thought her beauty could compete with Athena's?'

'Yes. Beautiful snake hair.'

'Yes, that was after Athena got to her … Envy is a terrible thing in a woman,' he laughs. He stops and puts his hand on yours. 'I want to tell you something, Theney. Don't distract me — it's hard enough as it is.' He is silent for a handful of heartbeats. It is very hard not to fill the empty space with rushing words. He finally begins again. 'I feel like I'm an old man.' He puts his hand up to stop you when he sees you open your mouth. 'Let me finish.' He pauses. 'I'm dead inside. My flame, my soul — it's fading. There's something about you.'

'No.' You want him to stop. You want to get up from the bench and get away from him. But then you look at him and see that you cannot leave. You must not.

He puts his hand in his jacket pocket, and he pulls out a small piece of paper.

'This is for you.'

It is a picture of you, in pencil, and he has drawn your face from the side, and he has made you look beautiful. There is a light around your face, a radiance to the skin. He has made you into an angel.

'When did you do this?'

'It's just a sketch.' But he wants you to say something.

'When did you do it?'

'Last night. I couldn't sleep …' A breath. 'Theney.'

You wait.

'I … It's …' He puts his elbows on his knees and buries his face in his hands. You rest your hand gently on his back, between the shoulder blades, and feel his body shake.

'She killed them both.'

'Shhh.' You feel a great fear. You desperately want him to stop. And you do not want to be here. You want to be in Linklatters drinking Shiraz. You want to be with the Princess, dancing to Abba. You want to go home. You want to run away.

'No, I want to tell you. I want to. I think I have to. My wife … I had no idea. She told me she was going up to Minneapolis to see her mother, and that night they were pulling her car out of the river. They wouldn't let me see the babies. I went mad with grief. I am still mad, I think. I … She … That tree, the golden tree — it's on the bend in the river where the car went in. We used to swim down there in the summer before we had the children, and since she died I've come up here so many times to think, to try to understand. But I don't understand. I can almost understand the suicide, but to kill the babies as well …'

There is nothing left for you to do. There is no choice, though a lump of nervousness has formed inside your stomach. But faced with this intensity of pain, this aching cry for help, your choices are removed. You turn his shoulders so he is looking at you, and putting your left hand under his chin you raise his head. He tries to look away but you do not let him. The thing you haven't felt for what seems like forever flows through you.

'Shhh,' you say quietly, 'it will be all right. You will be all right.' You put your right hand on your heart then touch the top of his head, where his silvery light shines most brightly. He is puzzled now, and watches your face. You sense a flicker of fear or uncertainty in his eyes. You move your hand to his heart, and you begin. It has been such a long time since the last time, but it is the only thing you can do right now. As you feel the exchange beginning, your strength into his warmth, his sadness into the space behind your heart, you feel the tears begin to well behind your eyes. This is your gift, and when you use it, you are complete. Yet this is also what makes you feel outcast, what you keep trying to escape. It is the truth of you, and you feel something like relief as whatever it is flows from your heart into his.

'What ...?' But before he can ask any questions you hush his lips with your hand. He is quiet. Not understanding, but accepting. Time stops, just like it always does. You continue until the exchange is complete.

When you are finished, you pull away. He reaches out to hold your hand, but you will not let him. You need to withdraw. He puts his hand on his own heart, and looks up at you, wondering.

'What ...? What did you ...?'

'I'm tired.' You start to walk slowly down the path, back the way you came. You feel so very weary. 'Take me home. Please.'

In the car, you curl up on the back seat. He is understandably worried.

'Are you all right?'

'Yes.' You try to smile at him reassurance. 'I just need to rest. Can you get me home?'

You do not hear his answer.

DOTTIE'S NOTEBOOK

The Princess became my next-door neighbour, but we rarely saw each other and we still had not become friends. I was still finding my feet here, learning how to live in snow and ice, far away from everything that was familiar.

And so, I am ashamed to say, with all this newness and all these uncertainties the need for alcohol began. Even with all the excitement and freshness of change, something was missing. Perhaps the emptiness was fed by my unrequited love for Daniel, left behind. Perhaps I just missed Dottie and her understanding. Perhaps I was just feeling sorry for myself. I found myself wishing just to be held, to be kissed, to have some eyes look into mine as though they liked what they saw; but these things do not happen just because a person asks them to. And since I also had a taste for gin and tonic, I was happy when one night I found a bar that made the best I'd had so far, served with lime, along with atmosphere and a bartender who did not immediately home in my Australian accent and act as though it was the most important thing about me.

He put out his hand and introduced himself. 'I'm Lloyd,' he said.

'Theney,' I replied and shook his hand. I told him my name once on that night and he never forgot it. It was one of the many good reasons to keep coming back to Linklatters.

I like Lloyd for many reasons. He is from Massachusetts and he says tomato like I do. I had taken a liking to him before I heard it, but when he said *'tomahto'* for the first time, that cemented it for me; cemented the sense that he was a type of kindred spirit. It has occurred to me more than once that if the way a person pronounces tomato can be this important then I am probably looking too hard for connections. A kindred spirit is should probably be recognisable for other kindred spirit attributes, rather than for the way they say the names of certain items of produce.

A place like Linklatters was good to find. It was the kind of place that could balance the solitude and quietness of the new life I was leading.

On that first night at the bar, I remember stamping my boots outside to shake the snow off, then walking inside and the few people there all turning to see me come in. Some things are so very different here. I am different here. I had done things like this in Australia — I often went to Lolita's Flamenco Bar by myself. But here I felt more fearless, somehow — fearless and waiting, almost breathless with excitement, for the next adventure to appear in my path.

A little sip of the gin and tonic that Lloyd served me and I looked around at the people who shared this place with me. A couple here, a quiet group there and, at the other end of the bar, a man who returned my glance with a smile. He had an outdoor look about him, dark curly hair, nice mouth, dressed casually but neat with very cool lace-up boots with chunky soles — I do love a man in a nice pair of work boots. Lloyd was talking to someone just a few seats up the bar in the other direction. I glanced up there, then took a second look. It was the Princess! I didn't want to interrupt their conversation and I needed to keep myself occupied. It was for this reason that I finally took out the notebook that Dottie had given me and, pen in hand, was finally ready to try to understand the past. It seemed the right thing to do — to document the chapter behind me as I started a brand new one. Besides, I owed it to Dottie. So I began. *'Dottie asked me to write this, and I somehow never started'* ...

I was about to finish the first drink and a second page when Lloyd appeared in front of me. With a sideways motion of his head, he indicated the man at the other end of the bar. 'The gentleman wants to buy you a drink.'

I was at a loss since this had never happened to me before. At thirty-one years of age, I was sure that I was not someone who had drinks bought for her — it was in fact unthinkable. I didn't get flowers or love poems. I dreamt of them, and sometimes wished, but there was something about me that prevented the advances that men made to softer women. After all, I had spent years building walls around myself to prevent me from touching people. And I'd accepted that walls work both ways. I accepted that.

I hesitated, then leant forward towards Lloyd and

nervously asked, while blushing, 'Ummm. When a person buys you a drink, what are you expected to do if you accept it?'

A tinkled laugh beside me and I looked up to see the Princess with her head on one side, looking at me. 'Hi, do you mind if I join you?'

'No, of course … Were you laughing at me? I mean …' Not sure how to put this, I ploughed on regardless. 'What else is being offered other than a drink?' I looked down, getting really embarrassed now. 'It's just that I've never had to do this before.'

Even Lloyd laughed then, a short laugh, but not unfriendly. 'You'll be all right Theney.'

The Princess smiled at me and leaned forward conspiratorially and I heard her Southern accent for the first time. 'You don't have to do anything you don't want to. If you like, you can thank him nicely and leave it at that. If you want to, you can ask him to join you. It's up to you, honey.'

I smiled with relief. 'Thanks. I'll accept the drink. And would you mind asking him if he'd like to join me? Us?'

The Princess smiled back at me, knowingly, in a way that made me feel that I was part of a sisterhood. 'That is an excellent idea. Let's make him sit right here between us,' patting the stool.

It seemed that Lloyd's message was just what the man at the bar had been waiting for, and he almost tipped his chair over to get to the two of us. I was grateful for his near accident. It made me feel less of a dork. 'Hi,' he said, when he finally reached where we were sitting. 'My name is Mark.'

'I'm Theney,' I said, 'and this is …'

The Princess cut me off. 'Very pleased to meet you, Mark.' She smiled. He turned to her, forgot I existed, and in this way my friendship with the Princess and my new life in Prospect both began.

PROSPECT

When you wake you are on the sofa downstairs in your apartment and it is dark and the clock on the video says 19:00. You are not sure if it is Saturday or Sunday night. It might even be Monday, though that would mean you had slept a record fifty-five hours. There is a note from Aubrey on the coffee table: *We need to talk. Please call.*And his number. You crush the scrap of paper in your hand and sit up on the sofa for a moment, indulging in the melodrama of resting your head in your hands.

After a few moments you notice your notebook on the coffee table, and you pick it up, flicking idly through the pages. You wrote down the past, but you're not sure if writing it down has helped you to understand anything. Nothing's changed because here you are, in a bigger fix than you have ever been in. You have been avoiding using your gift and yet it felt so right to be drawing the pain away from Aubrey. How will you manage these two conflicting urges — the one that makes you want to take a person's pain away and the one that makes you want to run away? Admittedly, it always does feel right to use the gift.

It's the issues that other people have with what you do that cause problems. And now you're faced with something bigger than the past. The present. You wish there was a book you could read, or someone to talk to. A Dottie, or someone like her. Suddenly, Prospect weighs heavy on your heart because it makes you feel so far away from home. You reach across and pick up the remote, flicking the TV on to the weather channel to see how it's looking out there in normal-land. It is still Saturday, which means you only slept about six hours. Perhaps you're stronger now than the last time you put your hand on someone's heart and took their pain away.

You go to your bookshelf and scan the spines for something to read, a world to escape to. You need instructions. A user manual. *Learning to Live with Your Gift*, or *Falling in Love With a Damaged Man — and Surviving the Experience.*

Time to go out and get drunk. Time to think about moving on. On the way out to the car, you see the lights are on in the Princess' apartment; but you don't stop to see if she wants to come out. You need to drink alone this evening.

Linklatters is busy. You hesitate at the door into the bar before walking in, nearly turning back. You are not sure you can face all those people. The thought of them is almost worse than the alternative of the sixth and ninth stairs in your apartment. But as you turn to go, a group of people comes up the path behind you and the man in front rushes up to you and opens the door, which means you would just appear rude if you turned and walked away. You smile your thanks and walk through the door into the familiarity of Linklatters bar with its warm lights and conversation.

Lloyd is working, which gives you a sense of relief mingled with wariness. You trust him, but today something changed. Past experience says that this afternoon with Aubrey has brought you to a place in your relationship with Prospect, Nebraska where you can start to say *'And things were never the same after that ...'*. Perhaps you should have called Aubrey before coming here. But somehow, you would not have known how to start that conversation. Perhaps it is too late, anyway. Perhaps Aubrey has already talked to Lloyd, had a cousinly chat.

A quick scan of the room reveals two empty seats at the bar. One would put you with your back to the door, so it is out of the question. The other one will do nicely. There are people in the way and you work your way through them; a few faces you have seen before and a few new ones. You return smiles, and say hello where it is expected. It is hard work to get where you are going and you realise that you are still very tired.

Lloyd has spotted you and nods at you with a smile. You sit and arrange yourself — the coat behind you over the back of your chair, your bag snugly against your thigh. You cross your right leg over your left leg and angle yourself into the chair. You made an effort with your clothes and make-up — it is a way of pretending that everything is all right.

'You look beautiful this evening,' says Lloyd.

'And you are a perfect gentleman,' you smile.

'The usual?' he asks.

You nod.

'You meeting someone? The Princess?'

'No,' you say. 'I just needed a change of pace. I think I might have an idea for a story.'

'To write?' asks Lloyd. 'You want to write a story? I thought you were more of a reader.'

You shrug. 'I am. I always was. But I feel like I need to write a story. A love story.'

'How are things with Aubrey?' he asks.

'Don't ask,' you say. Then, relenting, 'I don't really know.'

Before you can say more, there's a voice beside you. 'So you come in here quite often?' It is Robert, the Princess' new love.

'Hello,' you smile. 'This is a nice surprise.'

TRISTESSA AND LUCIDO

Lucido, master scribe and chronicler, whose name is the word for clear and bright in another language, had survived the long and bloody Demon Wars and suffered greatly for it. His lineage was a noble one and he had learned the art of chronicling as a child at the cedar desk of his father, who was also a great scribe, dedicating his life to recording the lives of kings and high-born men and women.

Lucido's gift as chronicler was evident even when he was a small boy. However, he did not write the stories only of noble men. Lucido wrote the stories of all men and women and believed that every human story was a jewel to be preserved. For many years, he chronicled the wars, and the lives of men and women who fought in them. The golden words that flowed onto his parchment captured human lives and loves so perfectly that a reader a thousand miles and as many years away could feel the precise emotions, imagine the very surroundings of the people whose stories Lucido wrote. He had a skill with forming words that seemed to provide a direct link between his subject and the reader.

Even his very first chronicles, which he produced under his father's guidance at the age of nine, were hailed by all who read them as inspired by angels. And as he grew, so did his gift, and by his gift his family prospered. When he was of age, he was married well to a woman who was beautiful in form and spirit and she bore him a son in their third year of happy union. All who knew Lucido valued him, whether they were noble or lower born. 'Lucido by name, Lucido by nature,' said all who knew him. And it seemed to everyone that his was a life to which no demon could ever have access. Lucido, they said, was truly blessed.

When Lucido was five, four years before he produced his first chronicle, a little girl was born in a simple village in a country far away, across the widest of the earth's seas. Her father was the village blacksmith and her mother was a gentle seamstress. Their baby girl came into the world quietly and her eyes seemed filled with tears, even from the first time she opened them. And her mother looked at the tiny face of her baby girl and decided she should be called Tristessa, an unusual name for a blacksmith's daughter, and the word for sadness in another language.

Just six hours later, Tristessa's mother closed her eyes and died, lost to her husband and her daughter for ever. And Tristessa, nursed by one of the village women, grew healthy and strong and was some considerable solace to her father, who loved his little girl like a princess. She was her father's only child and she became his constant companion in the smithy. Her little body grew wiry and strong as she helped her father with his trade. She had red hair and fair skin like her mother's and eyes as big as saucers that were often filled with tears she could not explain.

In that time, blacksmithing was a most noble profession. Tristessa's father was a good man, learnèd and travelled and wise. At his anvil, Tristessa learned about fire and metal. In the evenings, in their simple cottage, he taught her to read and write and she learned that the qualities of metal are similar to those of the human heart.

'Tristessa,' he said, 'we are all fashioned from different ores and when the gods made you, my little wise owl, they used crystals mined from the soil in sacred places.'

PROSPECT

Your senses are heightened after the exchange with Aubrey this afternoon, so when the phone at the bar rings you know that it is the Princess. And you know, without even looking at him, that Robert does not want to talk to her. Lloyd picks up the phone. 'Hey doll,' he says and winks at you. 'How's my sweetheart tonight? Where you at?' She must be in her usual form — he chuckles into the mouthpiece, and seems unable to drag himself away. But he has a bar to run. 'I have to go,' he says. 'Do you want to speak to Theney?'

Even from where you sit you can hear her voice chirping questions into the phone. Lloyd looks directly at Robert, then shakes his head. 'No, he isn't here right now, sweets. Here's Theney,' and he hands the phone to you. Robert is sitting right beside you and even if you didn't know for other reasons, you would know in an instant of seeing him that he doesn't want to talk to her. He is waggling his hands out in front of him and shaking his head and mouthing *'I'm not here'*. You look at him as though you do not comprehend. It makes him waggle more. Which cracks you up. You resist the temptation to put him out of his misery.

'Theney here.'

'Hi honey, what are you doing there? Who are you with?'

'Just came in for a drink. Are you coming down?'

'Well I can't,' she giggles, 'I'm having a little party in my apartment. Have you seen Bobby?'

'Bobby?' You look at Robert quizzically, pointing at the phone as if asking if he wants to talk to her.

'Mmmm hmmm, Robert, you know ...' She has champagne bubbles coming out her nose, you're guessing. Things start to fall into place in your head. You shoot Robert a look.

'Have you been drinking champagne?' you ask her.

'Mmmm.'

'Who have you got there?'

'Oh, some people. Do you want to talk to them?' a crash at her end, as she drops the phone. A man's voice, then the Princess breathlessly asking, 'Who wants to talk to Theney?'

'Princess!' She must have heard you — it certainly turned a few heads in Linklatters. You drop your head a little and try to talk in a normal voice. She is more drunk than you thought. 'Is there anyone there who isn't drunk?'

'No, honey, nobody at all! You can't come to this party unless you're tipsy!'

'Can you tell me who's there?'

'Well, there's Kevin. Say "hi," Kevin ...' You hear a

muffled 'Hello'. And then she goes on, breathlessly, 'And this is John. Say "hello" to Theney, John.'

'Hi,' says a deep voice.

'Hi.'

Then the Princess is back. 'Why don't you come over, Theney? Can you see Bobby there?'

You turn around in your seat so you can't see him. 'No, I can't see him right now. Do you want me to come over?'

'I'm having a wonderful time!' she says.

'Do you want to play yes/no?'

'Mmmm hmmm,' she says. 'I would love that.'

Yes/no is the game you play when she needs to tell you something but there is someone in the room preventing her from speaking openly. The game is supposed to work both ways, but you never seem to need to play, so you've become very good at asking questions and reading volumes of meaning into single syllables.

'Do you need me to rescue you?' You might as well get straight to the point.

'Y-e-e-e-s.'

'Are there more than two men there?'

'Uh uh, there are not.'

'Are there any women?'

'No.' She giggles but it's only punctuation, or alcohol. It doesn't mean she's having a good time.

'Have you met these men before tonight?'

'No.' Her voice has gone very quiet.

'I'll be there in ten minutes. Okay?'

'Okay.'

You hang up. 'Shit.'

Robert is hanging his head over his bourbon, looking miserable. Whatever it is, it feels to you like it's his fault. 'What do you know about this?' you demand of him.

'What?' He looks up.

You are angry with him, and with the Princess. You put your coat on with short jerky movements, take some money out of your purse and put it on the bar. Lloyd has his back to you, down the other end.

'She doesn't do stupid things without cause. Have you seen her tonight? Do you know who those two men are?'

He's just looking blank. Confused. This winds you up. You lose patience.

'Tell me what you know. Come on … Tell me in the car.'

He puts his hands up in front of himself again and shakes his head, fending you off. 'I'm not going anywhere with you. You're as crazy as she is.'

You can see suddenly how this must look to him. 'Okay.' You sit down and put your hand on his sleeve. 'I'm sorry. I'm just upset because she's my friend and she can do really idiotic things when she's upset and then I have to rescue her. And it makes it easier if I know what I'm walking into.'

'How long have you known her?' he asks.

'About a year. Now tell me. Please.'

'There were a bunch of us. Three,' he says. 'You know, I thought we were getting on fine. It was great. I don't know what she wants. What does she want?'

'First things first. Let's stick to this afternoon. Did you know the others?'

'Not really, they're like, friends of some people I work

with. We'd been hanging out. We were drinking. We met her at the gas station.' His voice trails off and then he says 'What does she want?'

You grab his shoulder. 'Concentrate, now. You're telling me about this afternoon.'

'She invited us back to her place.'

You can picture it. Picture the confusion for a new lover who is the victim of the Princess in action; the way she plays with the men in her life, setting them up and watching them teeter on some sort of edge. Yet every man in her life just keeps coming back for more. It makes you wonder what she does with them when nobody is watching. Or is there something in the game that works like an elastic band and keeps them snapping back to her?

'You went to her apartment?'

He nods. 'I don't know what to do. I've been thinking about her, on and off, since I knew her. I never expected to see her again. Everything's a mess.'

'Apparently,' you snort. 'But right now I think she might have got herself into a little situation. I'm going out there to see. Do you want to come?'

'No,' he finishes the rest of his drink in a gulp. 'But I will.'

'Good lad.' You help him on with his coat.

TRISTESSA AND LUCIDO

The blacksmith loved his daughter but he was a wise man and he could see, as Tristessa grew in skill and knowledge, that although she had been born into a humble home, she had a great destiny in store for her.

As she grew in years, she also grew in beauty and in fierceness. Tristessa had a warrior's heart and it made her father's own heart heavy to think about where a warrior's journey might take her. At the same time he was proud of her and knew that the best he could do as a father was to give her the things she would need to keep her strong.

In fact, Tristessa was more than a warrior. She had been born with a great gift. She could see demons where others could not, and she had the courage to rout them out. In those troubled times of the Demon Wars, warriors like Tristessa were sought out by the armies of light.

As she grew from childhood to womanhood, Tristessa began to realise that she had a responsibility to use her gift; but she did not yet know how and where to use it. Although there were demons everywhere, the Demon Wars were taking place in lands across the sea. People in her quiet village did not always appreciate Tristessa's ability to see demons, nor did they understand her desire to fight them. 'There have always been demons among us, and there always will,' said the people in the village. 'Let sleeping demons lie.'

At times it seemed to this young woman that what she had been born with was less a gift than a nuisance.

She continued to live a quiet life of discipline and learning at her father's side, believing it was her duty and that her time as a warrior would come. Meanwhile, with her father's help and somewhat in secret, she learned a warrior's skills. Her weapons were not fashioned from steel, nor from any sort of metal. She was no swordsman or archer. Her weapons were her mind, her heart and her instinct.

Under the guidance of her father, Tristessa learned that we are all warriors. Throughout our lives, we are presented with choices, and the paths down which these choices lead us are rarely easy. In fact, that is sometimes how we can tell which is the warrior's path. Warriors choose the thorns, choose the learning, choose the way that will grow their spirits and nurture their souls. Truly, life as a warrior can be troubled. If you look around, you will see many of us have laid down our arms and are resting, weighed down by tiredness, unable to go on, and are now taking the easy path.

PROSPECT

The roads are treacherous and Robert is silent in the car beside you. You are only a block away from Linklatters and as you turn into Elm Street, he wants to tell you what happened. 'I want to tell you what happened,' he says.

'If it's about you and her, I probably can't help.' You've learned to stay out of the Princess' relationship issues. They are too complex, and she weaves a treacherous web. If you were ever under the impression that life was easier for a man than for a woman, a few nights out with the Princess cured you of that naïve misapprehension.

Relenting, you say, 'You can tell me about it, if you like. But I can't promise to offer any advice. She's a mystery to me as well.'

'Does she have someone else in her life?'

'You'll have to ask her.'

'Oh God,' he says. 'Let me out.' He puts his hand on the door handle as though preparing to jump. 'I'm going to be sick.'

You pull over and he does what he has to do. You

don't want to rush him, these things take their own time; but you need to be sure that the Princess is all right. 'We have to go,' you say.

'No,' he shakes his head. 'You go. I live just around the corner.'

'Can I drop you?'

'No. I need to walk, I think.' He pauses, then takes a pen and a scrap of paper out of his jacket and writes his number down. 'You'll be okay. They're nice guys, but she … Look, call me if they give you any trouble.' He turns his collar up, and pushes his hands deep into his pockets and turns away.

You watch for a minute then roll the window down. 'Robert.'

He looks around.

'If you love her, she's probably worth it. If you don't she'll break you.'

He turns away and keeps walking. You pull away and head in the direction of home.

TRISTESSA AND LUCIDO

As long as there have been battles to fight, the best warriors have known that they must understand themselves and their enemies in equal measure.

Under her father's watchful eye, Tristessa learned about her enemy and she learned about herself. She learned first about her own demons, and the things she did that would invite them into her heart. She learned not to cry. Then she learned to cry again. She learned to fight. Then she learned how to win by not fighting. She learned when to be quiet and when to scream. Most of all she learned about love. This was the key to her power. It is the key to power for anyone whose aim is to dislodge demons from human hearts — whether it is from their own hearts or those of others — since above all other things, it is love which demons fear. In the fight against demons, a warrior is always beset. And yet love prevails, and it is our faith in it that makes us frail creatures so precious.

At the time of our story, Tristessa was by no means finished her learning. There are some lessons that are hard to learn, some skills that are difficult to obtain, especially if a warrior stays at home. Throughout her training, Tristessa lived with her father in their little village and worked with him in the smithy, growing in strength and restlessness.

Finally, on her seventeenth birthday, Tristessa's father sent her away.

'You are a warrior, and you are needed in the world,' he said to her. 'I fear that if I do not make you go, you will stay with me here until I die, and since I intend to live for many years, it may then be too late.' He smiled at the tears that had welled up in her eyes. 'Take your warrior heart and fight some battles in other lands. Learn from the world and help humankind. You will always be my little owl, with your eyes as big as saucers, and I love you.'

PROSPECT

When you get to the Princess' apartment, the lights are on and the front door is open. There is no one downstairs, and you run up to her bedroom calling her name. The bathroom door is closed. You knock and she calls out 'Theney?' She is sitting in the bath up to her neck in bubbles. Scented candles burn around the edges of the bath and on the floor around her.

'Where are your guests?'

'Oh,' she shrugs, 'they left a few minutes ago. I'd been trying to get them to leave for ever.'

'I saw Robert. He didn't seem very happy.'

'Where is he?' She half rises out of the bath.

'I dropped him off near his house. What happened?'

'He left. He was jealous. You know I can't stand it when a man gets jealous.'

'You drive them to it, you know.'

She picks up her champagne glass and downs the last mouthful. 'There's another bottle in the refrigerator. And you could get a glass. C'mon in Theney … I'm wearing a swimsuit.' She giggles.

'Did something happen between you and Robert?'

She eyes you. This is not a good time. It will be a waste of breath. She holds her left hand up then, and says like a pronouncement, 'Until I have a ring on this finger, I am free to do as I please.'

'Listen, I'm tired,' you tell her. 'I had a big day. I should sleep.' You turn to the door, but she says your name before you leave.

'Theney ...' She has that little girl tone. She's going to ask for something. 'Stay with me? I hate to be alone. Tell me a story.'

You suddenly realise. 'Why are you wearing your swimsuit? Were you in the bath with those men?'

'No,' she pouts. 'They were party poopers.' She sounds six years old. 'I thought a bath was a good idea,' she continues.

'I have to go. I'll talk to you tomorrow.' You shake your head and leave.

The nature of your friendship with the Princess would be hard to explain. You haven't really tried. After you have been home for about half an hour, you call her. Just to check she is all right. You make yourself a cup of tea, and settle on the sofa and dial.

'I'm so glad you called,' she sobs.

'Tell me,' you say, 'tell me what happened.' And she does.

Robert and the Princess had, in her mind at least, moved into the exclusively dating phase of courtship. It had been three weeks, and he had a crush on her ten years ago. But Robert, who seemed to be 'The Answer', has decided to take a step backwards from whatever spoken or unspoken decision he thinks he might have inadvertently made. He was married before and his story is that he is unsure of how much he has to offer. He is unsure of whether he can give her what he thinks she deserves. The upshot of it all is that he loves her but wants them both to keep seeing other people. He does say that he won't sleep with anyone else — just date them without the sex. Both of you know that that is not the point. She is devastated. She thought that Robert was a miracle. He has instead turned out to be too good to be true.

But the Princess you know does not hide for long behind sad tears and after an hour on the phone during which you try to be the best friend you can — offering to come over and have her stay at your place for the night — she is already planning how she is going to handle this and has decided that the relationship has to be exclusive or nothing and that she needs to find another boyfriend. You laugh out loud at her words, so relieved are you that the friend you knew is back, and soon you are planning the weekend. You will once again go out on Friday night and again on Saturday night if necessary to mend her heart with a new man. You will be her chaperone. You have done this before. You will help her sort through the many men she will attract, with her perfect hair and teeth and they way she carries herself as she walks into the room. You will be there to protect her if she gets too drunk to make sensible decisions. You will be there to tell obnoxious males to take a running leap. She promises she will not keep you out too late and that Linklatters will once again be your last stop so you can chat to Lloyd.

By the end of the phone call the two of you are planning what to wear and, despite your previous experiences, you are almost looking forward to the weekend's adventure. She flips her coin again, surprising you by wanting to know about you.

'And what about your day?' she asks. 'You said it was a big one.'

'Yeah,' you sigh. 'It was big.'

'Do you want to talk about it?'

But you decide against it.

TRISTESSA AND LUCIDO

In the third year of the greatest Demon War, Lucido's family was killed. As he wrote stories by lamplight in the tower room he loved to work in, a murderous party of enemy warriors broke into his home and slaughtered first his aged parents and then his wife and baby boy in their beds. And he, absorbed in his writing and unknowing, discovered their twisted, bloody bodies when he crept in quietly for fear of waking them, and thinking only of his wife's sweet smile and his baby son's burbling giggles.

Lucido's despair was great. But he was a good man, and had long since made his choices about light and darkness, so he did not immediately succumb to fear and anger. In truth, however, for the first time in his life, he was truly alone, and more vulnerable than he had ever felt before.

Lucido kept the demons away for as long as he could, and longer than many would have expected, but inevitably, time passed and the fight began to take its toll. Lucido withdrew. The light that had guided him in his writing seemed to him to be receding. He felt as though the fire that was the source of his gift and his strength was faltering. The flame at his centre wavered, threatened by the icy wind that began to freeze his heart and cloud the clear windows of his soul. People around

155

him looked at the ground when they talked about him and shook their heads in sadness. 'He is in pain,' they said.

And so it was that in his thirty-fifth year, two years after his family had been killed, Lucido turned his home into a fortress so that he could be safe from demons, not understanding that he carried the greatest demons with him. He fortified his home with stone and metal. He soundproofed the walls and roof so that he could hear no sound from outside, no sound of life or love. He shuttered the windows so thoroughly that not even a shard of daylight could reach him. If he wanted to see outside he had to open a big grey metal door with its seventeen locks and fasteners, or climb a hundred stairs to look out the windows of the tower room that had once been his work room, although he rarely went there any more. If it snowed outside, he did not know. If it was a hot sunny day, he did not know. He stayed inside his fortress and tried to keep his soul's flame alive all by himself — a task guaranteed to break the human heart into a million little pieces.

Lucido barricaded himself into his home and grew a little older and a little more sad with each year that passed. Sometimes he would accidentally catch a glimpse of his own face in the mirror and he saw an old, tired man. He began to dream himself dead or dying. He sought the comfort of alcohol to numb the pain of dying inside. Sometimes in his fortress he would look at nothing for hours, unable to put even a single mark on the paper, unable to chronicle any life in the face of his own deep despair.

Sometimes it felt as though there was nothing in his heart left to give.

PROSPECT

It is one of those winter nights when it hurts to breathe. The air is so cold it forms crystals as you draw it into your nostrils. The engine block will freeze unless you start the car from time to time. And although you would probably freeze before the engine block does, it is the engine that worries you more. The crystalline air makes you feel exposed and visible as you sit and watch the doorway to Aubrey's apartment. How you got here, how you made the decision, how you dressed and how you managed to get out onto the street without falling on the ice, then in the car and warming it up then driving to where he lives — how any or all of this occurred is a mystery. You are not even sure why you are here. You are, of course, aware that there is a label for what you are doing and it has a dirty feel to it. A label like 'stalking', for example, could be applied to someone who sits in a car outside the apartment of a man she barely knows and …

You don't expect to see him. And then the outside light comes on, and you see a bowed head emerge from the doorway, followed closely by the rest of Aubrey Meadows. You feel as though your car must have a bright light shining on it. If he just glances in your direction he will see you sitting here outside his apartment, for no good reason, in your freezing car. He is bent a little and looks around nervously. By some miracle he doesn't see you. Perhaps it is because you have frozen, mid-blink, acutely aware of how awkward your situation would be if anyone were to see you and ask what you were doing. You act under the same impulse as a rabbit in the headlights. Aubrey turns and pulls the door closed behind him, giving it a push to check that it's secure before turning to face the street. Then he stands for a minute, within the light's frosted circle and blinks like a creature from a cave until his eyes have adjusted to the night's black shadows and white light. He looks up and down the road, and sees no traffic. He doesn't see you, either.

He steps out with his hands buried in his coat pockets, his head burrowed deep into his collar and the scarf wrapped around his throat. He takes small fast steps that crunch on the re-frozen snow. He seems pursued. A broken trail of condensed exhalation follows him across the road. He stops suddenly when he reaches the door of the bar. Above him the neon sign blinks on and off. GIRLS! GIRLS! GIRLS! He turns to take one last anxious look over his shoulder before he enters and the door closes behind him.

You watch the door, waiting for him to reappear. It is a black door, painted in gloss, and seems from where you sit in semi-crystallised weirdness, to be impregnable. If this were Melbourne, there would have been a spruiker outside and a waft of music tempting passing punters to

158

enter. It is too cold here for spruikers or passers-by — though that doesn't seem to have stopped Aubrey. Or you, for that matter.

You do not turn the engine on, in case he should walk out the door and see you. You give yourself just one more minute, one more minute, and wonder what it would feel like to freeze to death.

There is movement. The big black door at the GIRLS! GIRLS! GIRLS! bar has opened. You can see Aubrey, and he has a girl on each arm. The three of them are laughing and holding on to each other and they each carry a bottle in a brown paper bag. A sudden wave of dizziness has you putting your hand to your forehead. Something in this scene shocks you — it is so unexpected. You remember suddenly the thing he said to you in Sanderson Forest. Hadn't he said he should stop drinking and whoring? Hadn't it stopped you short to hear those words? And why should you care? What Aubrey Meadows does is Aubrey Meadows' business.

You need to leave. You need to leave now. You wait, feeling sick, while the giggling threesome cross the road and enter his apartment block.

TRISTESSA AND LUCIDO

Meanwhile, Tristessa's journeys as a warrior took her far away from her home. She travelled from place to place and word of her victories against demons travelled before her so that in every place she went to, there were fights to fight and hearts to save. For nearly ten years, Tristessa travelled and lived alone, and she fiercely protected her solitude. But as years passed and the demands on her grew greater, she began to feel weary. She had the gift to see demons and the tools to fight them, but as she grew in strength she felt obliged to fight all demons that she encountered, including those that tried to infiltrate her own heart. We shall forgive her. She was too young, too inexperienced, to know that because the struggle must continue forever, it will also never end, and demons are a part of this world. Fighting indiscriminately is less noble than naïve, and if a warrior survives their first battles, they learn to pace themselves eventually.

It seemed to Tristessa that the thing to do was to find a place where she could rest awhile and renew her strength. She had seen that cities were the only places to be anonymous, and she chose to stop and rest for some time in the next large city she came to. It so happened that the following week she came to the city where Lucido lived. Without a moment's hesitation, Trist-

essa disappeared from view in the narrow winding streets and rented a room from an old artist woman who asked no questions of the sad young warrior who had come to her out of nowhere.

For many months Tristessa lived alone in the city. Without the constant action of warrior life she began, for the first time, to miss the guidance and wisdom of her father and the comfort of village life. Tristessa began to feel lonely and to wonder whether maybe it was not enough to be just a warrior.

She spoke to the old artist who had rented her the room and whom she had come to trust. 'I think I need something to help me heal,' she said. 'My soul is weary and I cannot seem to find the will to fight or even just to live any more. What should I do?'

'I don't have an answer, but I can tell you that it helps me to concentrate less upon my own weariness, and more upon the world. We are less significant and more precious than we know,' said the old woman. 'Like specks of dust, we dance in our beam of light, only visible when the light shines on us, swirled around and turned on our heads by things we don't understand.

'All I can share,' said the old woman, 'are my own discoveries. But you have to find your own dance, your own beam of light.' She paused. 'Perhaps I can teach you to paint,' she said. 'Painting helps me remember who I am.'

So, just as she had learned to work with metal in her father's smithy, Tristessa now learned to work with colour in the old woman's studio. Instead of lightening her heart, Tristessa found that painting just seemed to make her more troubled. She was weighed down by a feeling of being all alone in this strange place. Sometimes she was so weighed down she could not move. Her heart was leaden. Sometimes the muscles in her stomach ached from crying. She looked at lovers and families and could

161

see only the absence of human love in her own life. She stopped dreaming and hardly slept. She sought the numbness of drink. She questioned her own value, her ability to fight. She lost her way and experienced a darkness of the soul like never before.

She had thought it right to stop and rest in this place. She had hoped for a moment that if the old artist could teach her how to express herself with paint, then her confusion would disappear and her path would once again become clear. Instead the opposite was happening. 'Why am I here?' she asked. She looked into her heart and up to the sky and saw nothing to answer her sad questioning. Tristessa lost hope and purpose, and coming from somewhere nearby was the sound of evil demon laughter.

PROSPECT

Almost before the door to Aubrey's apartment is closed you are in Linklatters, though, once again, you don't know how you got there, and Lloyd is pouring you a drink. He wants to know what you are doing back here.

'What are you doing back here, anyway?' he says. 'I always guessed you couldn't resist me.' But your face must have given something away. 'Something's up, isn't it?'

You nod.

'Do you want to talk?'

At this point, you start to cry, which is not what you want to do. In fact, you would give almost anything not to cry right now.

And Lloyd, bless him, hands a pile of bar napkins over to you. 'We close in half an hour. I can leave the others to clean up. We can talk, if you want ... If I can help.'

You wonder how he got to be so sweet. 'Lloyd, how did you get to be so sweet? Thanks, but ...'

'Theney, I'm a bartender — and a friend. It's okay.' He can see you're not convinced. He touches your arm. 'Believe me, I've heard it all before.'

You doubt it. 'It's okay Lloyd. But thanks. Some other time, all right?'

When you have dried your tears, you reach into your bag, take out the notebook you have been carrying around with you, and read through the beginnings of the story you have started to write about these two strange characters Tristessa and Lucido who came to you out of nowhere.

You don't want to burden Lloyd. And you don't want to take the consequences of telling him anything. Secrets, released, are destructive. They're secrets for a reason. Freed from their secret state, they are corrosive and they eat away at who you are because who you are is partly what you see reflected in the faces of those who look at you. And secrets can change what people see. A change that has nothing to do with who you really are.

So here you sit, at that green marble bar at Linklatters, with your pen poised over a page in your notebook, preparing to write another chapter in the story that is quickly turning into as much of an escape as any story you have read. You had no idea that writing was a way of escaping as well. Perhaps this is what Dottie was trying to lead you to.

You're no longer writing in the notebook that Dottie gave you. You've kept that as a place to document the past, and this story seemed to demand its own place.

The notebook you use for *Tristessa and Lucido* is one you bought when you first landed in America. You bought it at a bookshop and you told yourself that you would use it to record the journey to San Antonio, where you guessed you would make contact somehow with your aunt's spirit or some remnant of her and things would start to feel all right or at the very least fall into place. This notebook has Gustav Klimt's 'The Kiss' on front and back covers. At first you liked the size of the book and the spacing between the lines and the narrow spiral binding that would not damage anything else in your overstuffed handbag. And then in one of your reflective moments — or maybe it was just the Shiraz — you saw that the picture was a dream, and all you could really see of the man and the woman were faces and hands, surrounded by a whirling shower of love — if an orgasm could be painted it would probably look like this.

So in this notebook that has a picture of passion and belonging on its cover, you write this strange love story that has come to you from nowhere. It seems you've made yourself a little set of symbols.

And then, on some impulse, you put your pen down and ask Lloyd if you can use the Linklatters phone. He brings it to you and watches as you dial Aubrey's number.

TRISTESSA AND LUCIDO

For years Lucido stayed in his fortress and created his wondrous works, played music, read books and thought his thoughts and yet could find no peace. The people around him began to say, 'He is too hard to understand.'

'He pushes us away and sometimes he ignores us.'

'He needs to move on from his pain and start to live again.'

Sometimes he recognised that he dwelled too much on the harm that had been inflicted and not quite enough on the good things that life had given him; but he shrugged his shoulders at the stray thought and tried to convince himself that he had to accept what he had begun to view as his lot in life.

You see, in these difficult times, in the last years of the Demon Wars and the time that followed, many people believed that happiness was a goal towards which everybody should strive. But Lucido knew another truth — one that he understood from sad experience. He knew that happiness is an illusory prize, and exists for only fleeting moments, and can be transformed in one horrific instant to something more painful to remember. And this is what his demons preyed upon, for Lucido was both yearning to be happy and fearful of happiness at the same time, not understanding that even a fleeting moment can bring gifts that remain with you long after the moment has passed. Lucido was a loving man who had allowed himself to be so devastated by life that he thought he could never love again. And he was also an intelligent man who knew that every link in the armour he built around himself was keeping his heart in a form of stasis that carried its own hurt, and he sometimes doubted his choice to withdraw from the world.

With such confusion in their tortured host, with such a fertile imagination working in their favour, how could his demons, resting at the portals of the places where his darkest fears resided, how could they not be content, and even a little gleeful, at the prospects promised by such easy prey.

As Lucido survived, he tried to remain focused on the search for truth, the choice of light over dark. He held desperately onto the belief that he could one day find some peace. Yet it began to look as though the demons had found a way to win because he had forgotten that he had a right to joy and love and happiness. He was so tired that he forgot the reasons he had chosen the light over the dark for all those years. He forgot that we are all fierce warriors with the power to send demons wailing back to where they came from. He lost hope.

PROSPECT

The following afternoon, at the agreed time, you are knocking at his door. If asked, you would not be able to say why you are here.

The door opens. 'Come in,' Aubrey says quietly. 'I'm glad you called last night. Drink?' He tinkles his cup at you. 'Vodka and 7UP is all I've got.'

You shake your head. 'No, thanks.'

The apartment looks bigger without a party in it — an empty space that isn't cold, but seems as though it should be.

He takes your coat and indicates a tattered couch, then notices the things strewn across it and leaps across the room to reach it before you do, to straighten the covers, brush bits and pieces of fluff and lint onto the floor. 'I guess this proves I'm a bachelor,' he laughs. To which you have no response.

It is tricky to know how to sit. It is one of those old sofas that welcomes you in and will not let you go. The only way to deal with sofas like this one is to lie on them, and put your head on the arm at one end. But this is not the time.

You sit at one end and Aubrey stands in front of you and asks again, 'Drink?'

You've already declined once, but are glad for the opportunity to change your mind. When you nod now, it seems to make him happy. He almost runs to the kitchen area to start breaking ice into a blue mug for you. 'I only have cups,' he says. 'More evidence.'

'Of what?'

'Of my solitary status.'

'Oh.'

He wants to know if you are all right. 'You all right?' he asks.

'Why wouldn't I be?' Which is a stupid thing to say because it sounds as though it comes from some well of bitterness, and he has no idea that you were watching last night and saw what you saw. So you try to recover from the transparency of your question's nasty undertones. 'I'm just a bit tired.'

When the drink is made he brings it over to you and then sits opposite you in a tattered office chair with wheels, wheeling towards you, then away, towards, then away as if studying you.

You hold your cup up. 'Cheers.'

After drinking, he says, 'Can I ask you about what happened in Sanderson Forest?'

'I'd rather you didn't.'

'Right. I guessed you'd say that.'

'So why did you ask?'

'Doesn't hurt to try.' A pause. 'Can I play you something?'

You nod and he picks up the flute that sits beside him on the low table and starts to play. A beautiful tune.

'What's it called?' you ask when he's finished.

'I don't know yet,' he says. 'I think it might be part of something bigger. I've been taking the flute to the forest and playing it out there. It sounds great among the trees, particularly in the winter with snow all around. The snow does something to the sound.'

The sketches and photos stuck on one of the walls attract your attention again, like last time you were here. You remember seeing them when you came here for the party. He sees where you're looking.

'Take a closer look if you like,' he invites. Up close, you see that some faces are familiar, then you recognise the women you saw with him, coming out of the bar.

You point at them and ask 'Who are they?'

His look is sharp. Is he on to you? Did he see you sitting in the car and watching? 'Just a couple of strippers I picked up at the bar across the road. I want to use their faces for those angel sketches I'm doing. It's silly. A silly little obsession.' And then … 'Why are you asking?'

'I think I've seen them before.' And you step away from the wall.

'I doubt it. I can't imagine you in the same room with them.'

What sorts of judgements is he making? 'Was there a reason you chose to put strippers' faces on angels? Are you trying to make a point?'

He walks over to stand beside you. 'If you have to ask that, you're not as clever as I thought you were.' Which stings you. And then he says, 'They're whores.'

170

'I could be a whore, for the right reasons.'

There is silence in the room for a few seconds. A couple of times you think you might have something else to say but stop between opening your mouth and speaking. You and Aubrey stand side by side looking at the picture and something happens — a whirlpool of compassion for him makes you reach out to the wall to steady yourself. He does not see it though, because he is busy trying to escape from this thing that he has started.

'I made a mistake,' he says. 'This is hopeless. I shouldn't have started anything with you.'

'Don't worry,' you say. 'You didn't.' Even though you know he did. Somehow.

'Here,' he says. 'Seeing as you're here, should we listen to some music? Or do you want to go to dinner?'

'Let's do both.'

Was this really happening or were you simply imagining a quickening between you and Aubrey Meadows? Were you living in your own world or an unwilling participant in his? Perhaps a part of you that you can't acknowledge asked for him, or someone like him — someone difficult, and damaged, someone whom you could touch. Someone to drive the memories of Daniel away and give you something other than your own problems to think about. Someone to make this gift you have make sense. You put the call out, broadcast on the lonely wavelength, shouted to the foreign sky 'turn me around and give me purpose' and here he is, in Prospect where you came to answer the call. You know you did, and so it's easy to think that this may be the reason you are

171

here and yet ... none of this is formed quite this way in your head. The words miss the point by being words. All this is just the way it is. Yet something clicks.

And tonight, the two of you have to go out, and what else could you do, since you 'had to eat' (his words); so after just a little drink you go out to eat, he takes you to an Italian restaurant that he knows. As you walk in, he looks around and mutters 'Good, no one here I know', which further clouds the muddied waters. What is he afraid of? Is it a fear of being seen with you or a fear of being seen at all? The two of you do the circling thing; it is inevitable simply because you are, by accident, on a date and what else should you do but circle and try to find out things. Despite yourself, you begin to relax a few minutes into the garlic bread.

Later in his home, he pulls a CD off the shelf and plays it for you and says he wrote the songs when he and his wife were first in love. He says the music is mediocre, mawkish and mediocre. But you think he is too hard on himself, and tell him so. He squeezes your hand in his and sits you down in a chair, telling you not to move as he starts to draw your face. But you can sit only for a little while. You stand and he sits looking at you, frozen, with his pencil poised above the page. You do not speak. You walk across the room and it takes forever and a day to walk the distance of a metre or two and put your arms around his shoulders, your face in his neck, and without a shred of common sense, you pass the things you feel from your heart to his heart through your two not-so-separate skins and bones and flesh.

'Do you want to stay?' he asks, after some moments.

'I don't …'

'Don't worry. I just want to sleep …'

'That's not …' This has to stop. You have to stop it. 'Aubrey.' He stops and looks at you. There must have been something in your voice.

You kiss him on the forehead and you say, 'You said it yourself, it would never work.'

And you leave. He does not even get up from his chair. He looks at you as though you are an alien in his home. He watches you as you put on your coat. You turn and look at him before you walk through his door and your eyes lock with something in his and for a moment there is no way either of you can pull away. But then you find it in yourself and you are gone.

At home, you dial his number. He does not pick up and you cannot (will not) leave a voicemail for him since you don't know what to say, so you write a note and tell him thanks for dinner, then put the note in the rubbish bin.

You need to get away. And you need someone to talk to. You will call the Princess in the morning and see what she has to say. And after you have done that, you think that you will go, finally, to San Antonio.

TRISTESSA AND LUCIDO

One night, the old artist woman took Tristessa to hear Lucido at one of his rare readings. 'He is a great man, or he was,' she said. 'I think you need to hear his voice.'

The room was full. People from all over the city had come to hear him read his latest work. Something in Lucido's voice touched Tristessa. His stories were like nothing she had heard before and when he had finished reading, she approached and thanked him.

He smiled at her and as the room emptied around them they talked and talked. When Tristessa's old landlady finally convinced Tristessa to leave, Lucido would not let her go until she had agreed to meet him again. Soon they were seeing each other nearly every day.

It did not take long for Tristessa to think that perhaps Lucido had appeared in her life with some sort of gift or message for her. In her time of darkness in this new city, she had gradually withdrawn, and when Lucido met her she felt beaten and lifeless. She had hardened her heart to deflect pain, building a fortress inside her in the same way that Lucido had fortified his house. She had forgotten the big lessons of love — that it needs to be given with no expectation of return; that love generates love.

And that kindness and caring are the gifts given to all of us for constant distribution. On that first night, Tristessa noticed Lucido was filled with light. And indeed, when Lucido and Tristessa met, a door opened in their two separate hearts and they were both surprised.

And so began a time of great difficulty for both Lucido and Tristessa. For though she carried a great gift and he was a master chronicler, they were both frail human beings. And while they had both fought demons with varying degrees of success, their victories had not affected them as profoundly as their losses, and they were both fearful.

Tristessa knew soon after she met Lucido that this was a man who could get under her skin and break her heart with his smile and his eyes and his hands and the way he looked at her with his head on one side. She wasn't sure that this was what she wanted.

Lucido knew as soon as he said his first goodbye to her that this was a woman who could invade his fortress successfully, with her warrior heart and her belief in love. Something fresh about Tristessa, something he had never seen before, was stirring his heart in ways he did not wish to be stirred.

They carried on in fear of each other and yet, somehow, they could not let go completely.

PROSPECT

Given the day's events, it is no surprise that this turns out to be a night when, lying on your back and staring at the leafless shadows on the ceiling, you question who you are and what you are doing. The search for sleep is a fruitless one. Perhaps a whiskey, or perhaps some hot milk, or perhaps a combination. You persist in your efforts to sleep without help for about an hour. It's two in the morning when you give up, get out of bed and go downstairs to the kitchen.

The churning in your stomach is making it hard to concentrate on anything. You think perhaps you should watch television and dull yourself that way. More than once you have slept on the sofa downstairs, fully dressed, in an effort to trick yourself to sleep. The act of undressing and getting under the covers upstairs has a tendency to give the game up and leave you vulnerable to insomnia.

Tonight, there is nothing on the television that even vaguely distracts you. Common sense says you should do some yoga or something like it to calm your mind. But common sense, you know, can be overrated. After lying on the sofa for only a few minutes with the television off and the remote control in your hand, and your warm milk untouched beside you, something draws you to your notebook and the story you've been writing. It is a funny thing, you think, how nothing seems to be simple once you start to look beyond the surface.

It is becoming clear that your attempts to escape by travelling to Prospect and re-inventing yourself are not going as well as you had hoped. Stepping inside your front door when you come home from work or Linklatters, or wherever else you spend your time, becomes more difficult. Your chest tightens and you can actually feel your heart-rate increase. You don't know why; your home is supposed to be a safe place, but something about it makes you panic. Perhaps it is the fact that once inside the door there's no denying that you are alone. Perhaps it is something else. Analysis, in your experience, is not a great help.

Usually, the only thing that helps is reading. In the pages of other people's books you can live in realities — realities that often make more sense than yours does. But now you find yourself compelled to write this story. And you know the story is about Aubrey and what he means — somehow this story is about that. What does he mean? What should he mean to you? Something about Aubrey both requires and defies understanding. He has touched you. It is 'Aubrey restlessness' that has you picking up your pen and opening a fresh page, hoping that what you write will somehow reveal a meaning behind what's happening. You think about the collage on his wall, his sad face looking out from it. You remem-

ber the question he asked you about angels and you start
to write.

TRISTESSA AND LUCIDO

Lucido behaved like a wild creature, warily circling this new occurrence in his life and then withdrawing, approaching and pulling back. He told Tristessa more than once during this time that she should stay away.

'I am damaged,' he said. 'Do not attach yourself to me. I am a dying man.'

Whenever he spoke like this, Tristessa's eyes would fill with sadness and the demons nestled both in her heart and Lucido's would smile evilly to themselves.

Every time Lucido met Tristessa, he saw in her a promise of happiness that his bitter experience told him was a lie. And in the end it was easier to stay away than to make himself be with her. What was not easy was the fear he felt each time he saw her. He began to despise himself. He began to wish that they had never met. His fear was like an icy grip around his heart and it seemed that the best thing he could do was to avoid any contact with this disturbing woman. He could see that she needed only a small measure of encouragement and she would keep knocking at his armoured door, and he knew that a part of him could not resist the knocking.

From where he sat behind the armour, Lucido heard the

179

whispered reminders that love would be dangerous and could only lead to dashed hopes and broken promises. His demons prepared their weapons, spitting on them and sharpening their jagged edges. Even his knowledge of his own cowardice was salt in the wounds that he had already encouraged his demons to inflict. And then, a little bit at a time, he began to be angry at Tristessa, to hate her and to flinch away from every gesture of affection, every tone of admiration in her speech. And thus the battle was engendered

After years of hiding from the world, Lucido found himself once again reaching out to other people. Somehow, Tristessa had woken up the parts of him that he thought he had put to sleep forever. He went for long walks in the city and began to write again. He stayed out late at taverns and sometimes he took women home with him. Sometimes they went with him because they were flattered by the attention of the great chronicler, and sometimes they went with him out of pity, because they could see the sadness he carried. And although he tried to stop seeing Tristessa, he still he thought about her. Alone in his fortress, he hated her. When he saw her, he avoided and ignored her.

PROSPECT

The official paperwork says that you are here in this foreign town for work and no other reason, and even though you like your job, you know the paperwork is wrong. Something had you saying 'Yes' to Prospect, Nebraska even though there was no practical need for you to be here. It's not as though you need the money. In fact, if you should be anywhere, it should be in San Antonio. Rationally, that is where you should be.

The paperwork says that if you were to stop work you would have to leave Prospect and the USA. You are an alien here, in official terminology. You are bundled in with Martians and with Mexicans, neither of whom you resemble in the slightest (you suppose).

Susceptible to a somewhat questionable sense of logic, you feel sometimes that some things just have to happen. It's not fate or destiny so much as science — this gift of extrasensory perception plus that death of a relative with associated estate in America that needs taking care of plus these other unpredictable variables equals this miracle or gaping wound. Some things just have to happen.

Sometimes, you just have to let them. That's how you

came here, to the Mid-West of America, to watch the snow outside your kitchen window, watch the pretty snowflakes and automatically link them in your head with all the things you know are their natural consequences. You will have to sweep and scrape them off your windscreen. You will have to wear your snowboots to the car on Monday morning because the apartment maintenance man will not have had time to clear the path by the time you leave for work. You will hear the words "winter wonderland" emanating from people who do not understand that the pleasure of alliteration ultimately gives way to impatience at the mindless repetition of the trite phrase. You will be asked again, and again, as a foreigner from a country they all think is paradise, whether you are enjoying this snowy spectacle. And perhaps to someone from Prospect, Nebraska, Australia could be paradise, just because it does not snow on all the city streets there, and cover the place with freezing whiteness that can, after a lifetime, grow tedious.

A few nights later you expand on this at Linklatters as you sit drinking your Shiraz. You say 'Free will is all very well,' to anyone who will listen, knowing that someone will, even if it is only Lloyd or a regular who will swivel his head around with bleary eyes and recognise and dismiss you in one complete gesture. On this occasion, though, the someone who listens is an unsuspecting traveller, here in town for a few nights on business. He came to Linklatters as so many of them do, to check out the action.

He is, you admit, perfectly groomed. You wonder whether his hair is real or a toupee. He starts the conversation by asking whether you are British. Same old question. Nothing wrong with being British, you suppose, except that it is something you are not and, after a year here, you sometimes have trouble responding in a friendly way to that harmless mistake. Inside your head, you roll your eyes, but outside, on your face, you smile and say laconically, 'No. Australian.'

A gentle smile, one that you hope will not offend. It is so easy to offend here, and you are, after all, supposed to be a gentle female creature pleased that he has singled you out; so you must try extra hard to be nice to him so as not to hurt anybody's sensibilities. The rule is lots of smiles and no swearing. Whatsoever. You brace yourself now for whichever one of the three standard follow-up statements he will deliver in response to the information you have just given him about your nationality.

'Australia!' he says excitedly. 'Y'know I've always wanted to go there.'

This is by far the most common of the three responses. You are not drunk and he seems quite nice and you are lonely for company so you look at him and smile sweetly.

'You should go there one day,' you say. 'You would probably have a fabulous time.'

He laughs and repeats the word. '*Fabulous,*' he says. 'You know, I love your accent. I could just listen to you talk all day long.'

It seems like the right moment to try a gentle dig and test his sense of humour quotient. 'It probably wouldn't even matter what I said, right?' You look up at him in a way that you hope appears coy, and smile sweetly, laughing your head off on the inside.

And ouch, here it comes … He says nothing, then laughs nervously. You console yourself with the thought that he is at least easy on the eye and maybe he has an intelligent friend.

Soon he is buying you a drink and asking, 'What do you think about American men?'

You look at him again. He is perfectly nice, nicely perfect. Well groomed, with a ring on his little finger, but no wedding ring, or at least not on the wedding finger. He seems genuinely interested and you have a choice now. You can choose to assume that he really wants to know, or you can assume that he wants to hear something flattering.

You are not drunk, but have enough Shiraz in you, have lived long enough alone in this nothingness, that you will choose the path of flattery if only to keep him looking at you for just a few more minutes. You want the attention. You make a mistake. You tell him something insipid, something not true, something polite and pleasant about American men; and just before you get to the end of the sentence, the door to Linklatters opens and a group of perfect women walk in, accompanied by a group of satisfied men whose number is one less than the number of women. You can feel his attention wander; like strings of home-made toffee, the threads of your conversation stretch until they are too thin to support themselves. They break, finally, and he has turned his head completely towards the newcomers.

You have lost him to their perfect hair, their American

teeth, the dependable safeness of their polished, sharpened nails and the layer of make-up on their perfect desirable faces. They talk amongst themselves as they decide on a place to perch and it sounds to you like a flock of cockatoos, screeching as they fly into the valley to roost the night on the tall gum trees down by the creek of your childhood.

He excuses himself and says he knows one of the men who has just walked in. He picks up his drink and goes over to the other side of the bar where the flock is smoothing its feathers and asking for menus. He shakes hands and stands chatting for a while. He does not come back and your feel your shoulders rounding and your eyes filling with self-pity as your face drops closer to the Shiraz saviour in the glass. The Princess would say that there's an easy way to deal with this. She is a polished creature too, though not the kind who brings to mind a screeching cockatoo. But if you want something, and you know how to get it, then do whatever it takes, she would say. Whatever it takes. And when you say goodbye to Lloyd an hour or so later, the guy is chatting warmly and intimately to one of the cockatoo women. She holds her cigarette up to be lit then draws smoke from it and lifts her face to blow it out again provocatively. You should have told the guy what you really think about American men.

Driving home alone you feel it again, that wailing *why* in your throat, behind your eyes, and the spasms in your stomach that make it hard to breathe.

You think to yourself that this could have a cumulative effect, all this wanting love and never getting it. You either need to stop wanting it or you need to get some, but you can't imagine Theney not wanting love and meanwhile you are alone and you live your life alone and it feels as though life lived alone is not worth living. Of that you are almost completely sure. You know with certainty that you are not separate from those things that surround you and yet at the same time you feel terminally separate.

The world outside you includes other people, but there are walls between you and them. Aubrey for example. You accept responsibility for having built the walls, and you know you are responsible for maintaining them too. And now the walls are so much part of who you are, and you are so fearful of the consequences should you break them down, that you are stuck and what has happened with Aubrey and what just happened tonight will keep happening, again and again, until you can break free. Somewhere deep inside you are the tools you misplaced some time ago — tools you could use to break down the walls so that you can re-connect.

So you drive home, and even though it is snowy, you take risks. You drive fast in your little car, too fast to be able to stop if you had to. You don't want to put anyone else's life in danger but you want to take some risks with your own, which seems to be meaningless right now. You didn't even want that man but it would have been nice to be the one to choose. Automatically using clutch and brake, changing up gears and down again and widely swerving, thankful for the late-night-stay-at-home-and-rent-a-video-and-order-in-pizza emptiness of the roads, you make it home. And you sit in the car on the side of the snowy street with the lights off and the engine slowly freezing and hope that no poor fool is walking by to see the sobbing.

TRISTESSA AND LUCIDO

Despite all her warrior experience, Tristessa was unused to the ways of demons as sophisticated as those that Lucido harboured; and her judgement was clouded by emotions she had never experienced, and did not understand. She believed that every time he pushed her away, he was testing her, unconsciously or not, and that she could pass this test only with steadfastness and loyalty and unconditional acceptance. She knew his pain was greater than her own. She also felt that this man was important to her. He had not come into her life by accident, of that she was sure.

And truly, since meeting Lucido her life had begun to improve. As a warrior she had felt shielded and guided by a sense of purpose, by the part she played in the fight against demons. And then, in her first dark months in the city, all that clear sense of herself had fallen away. Now, since meeting Lucido, she had started sleeping and dreaming again. She had broken off her numbing friendship with drink. Clear messages about him came to her in dreams.

Even though they saw each other rarely, with Lucido in her life, Tristessa's strength returned and whenever she saw him, whether in his fortress, or in a street or at a gathering, she felt as though she were coming home. It made no sense to her that he could not feel it too. She could not understand the way he pushed her away.

Meanwhile, Lucido's life took another turn. It was true that he had begun to open doors that had been closed for years, but his demons would not give him up so easily. He began to drink enough each day to numb his feelings, and could not work as a consequence. He tried to sleep and imagined he heard voices telling him he was a fool. His stomach hated him and he could not eat except to have the food he swallowed leave his body, rejected almost immediately. He thought about Tristessa all the time, then cursed his feelings and the confusion they created.

And thus can demons prey on a person and leave them feeling cursed when a small and regular dose of love and courage would cure their illness for all time.

PROSPECT

Even first thing in the morning, the Princess is beautiful. Rumpled and bedraggled with her blonde hair all mussed and sleep in her eyes, she has an adorable little girl-ness that reminds you why you always feel the need to protect her.

'Good morning,' you say brightly.

'Coffee?' is her response. She has a pot ready, and in a minute or two you are sitting in a patch of winter sunshine in the front room of her apartment and it strikes you that this is a perfect moment.

'This is a perfect moment,' you say.

She smiles and takes a ladylike sip from her cup before ruining the morning air by lighting a cigarette. Perfection goes up in smoke. You grimace and she shifts so the smoke is not blowing right at you.

'Sorry.'

''S okay.' Which of course it isn't, but you say it anyway. And then you start again. 'I have to tell you something, but you have to promise ...' You pause. There's a piece of lint on your pants. You pick it up and roll it between your fingers until it is a tiny ball.

'What?' she says. 'Just tell me.'

'Even when I was very small, I could see things. I knew things.' It's a long time since you tried to talk to anyone about it, and the words don't seem right.

But the Princess interrupts, almost impatiently. 'Did he tell you yet?'

'Did who tell me what?'

'Did Aubrey tell you what happened with his wife?'

'He told me she died, and he mentioned the babies.'

'Well, do you want to hear the whole thing? Everybody knows the story.'

'Tell me then.' The Princess loves a story.

'Well,' and she takes a big drag on her cigarette to build suspense, which irritates you. But you say nothing. 'They were sweethearts in high school, and they were married when she was twenty-one and he was twenty-two. They tried to have children for years, but they couldn't. She told me once that he didn't mind. He was so wrapped up in his music. He always said that jazz musicians are too self-centred to have families and he wasn't convinced he had anything left over to give to children. But then they went on one of those programmes, you know, the fertility programmes, and then she was pregnant. But at about that time, she started to act a bit strange. There were all sorts of rumours flying around.' The Princess leans forward conspiratorially. 'They say she had AIDS when she died.'

'Who says? Did she get it from Aubrey?'

'Well, there's a story about that too ...'

There is movement on the stairs and you look questioningly at the Princess. She giggles, covering her mouth with her hand. 'Robert? Is that you, Bobby?'

Robert puts his head around the corner sheepishly. 'Morning Theney.'

'Good morning to you, too.' You arch an eyebrow at the Princess. 'Do you want me to go?'

'No, of course not. Bobby, honey, do you want some coffee?'

'Yes, but it's okay, I'll get it. You girls go on chatting.' He pads into the kitchen.

'Anything you want to talk to me about?' you ask.

'Yes, later,' she says. 'When he's gone. Let me finish the story now.'

'What story?' asks Robert, coming out of the kitchen with his coffee and the pot to fill your cups.

'You know, what we were talking about last night.'

'Oh, Aubrey Meadows. You know Theney, he's a weirdo.'

'Bobby, leave her alone.'

'Can you please finish the story?' you ask, worried that it will slip away, now that you are finally interested.

'Well, there's nothing to tell, really. She had twins and when they were born, they were HIV positive, just like her.' The Princess leans towards you, excited to be sharing this information. 'She had given it to them, you know, in the womb.' She shudders then takes another drag on her cigarette, for dramatic emphasis this time. She blows the smoke away from you but the draft from the central heating wafts it back.

'That's terrible ... And Aubrey?'

'Well, that's the thing. It turned out they weren't his.

192

She'd been having this thing with some farmer she met at the stop lights on 90th and Elm one day. Turns out he gave it to her, and the twins were his, and anyway she couldn't stand it and committed suicide and took the twins with her.'

'Stop lights? You mean traffic lights?' You feel as though you are sinking into some sort of morass, deeper and deeper into some weird place where all the threads of the story are disentangling and floating off, the opposite of what a story should do.

'Is that what you call them? Traffic lights? How cool is that?' The Princess giggles.

'She was a stripper,' says Robert, thankfully ignoring this red herring. 'That's how they survived during those years when he wasn't getting many gigs, and all he had was a few students. He hated it.'

'He would throw these amazing rages,' says the Princess. 'Ask Lloyd one day. He's had to save the situation more than once.'

You see, suddenly, what a small town is Prospect, Nebraska.

'Yeah,' says Robert, 'and then when she has a fling it's not with a customer, it's with some guy at the stop lights.'

'So what happened?' you ask.

'Well, she told me one night at Linklatters,' says the Princess, 'before she fell pregnant. She was really drunk. She made me swear not to tell. She was at the stop lights and there was this really cute guy in a pickup beside her. He kept trying to catch her eye. She said he was really good looking. Anyway, she was going to Maple View Mall, and she parked her car and went inside, and then when she came back there was this note on the car windshield and a red rose. He told her she was the most beautiful woman he'd ever seen and he told her his number. She said that Aubrey was never romantic like that. She thought it was so wonderful.' The Princess rolls her eyes. She obviously doesn't think much of the gesture.

'Then one day she and Aubrey had a fight,' Robert cuts in, 'and she stormed out and booked into a motel and called the guy.'

'Can you believe that?' The Princess acts incredulous.

'Well,' you say slowly, 'I guess that's an interesting story, but who knows if it's true. It could all just be made up.'

'Ask Lloyd,' says Robert.

'Ask Aubrey,' says the Princess.

'It's no wonder he's fucked in the head,' says Robert and the Princess throws him a look.

You change the subject. 'Will you give me a lift to the airport tomorrow?' you ask her. In response to her questioning look, you simply say, 'I'll call you later. Nice to see you again, Robert.'

They smile at you — the perfect couple — and you leave them to it and go next door to get your coat.

TRISTESSA AND LUCIDO

One day Lucido saw Tristessa in the street and he said to her, 'Please come to dinner with me. We have to talk about this thing between us. You are ruining my life.'

She agreed to meet him and they went to one of the places they had discovered together when they first met, when he had not yet started to push her away. He could not talk. The silence between them was awkward and he covered his discomfort by drinking too much wine. Her heart sank as she watched him finish glass after glass. Eventually, the alcohol numbed not only his discomfort but his fear as well. Instead of being angry with her and telling her to stay away he kissed her and she kissed him back. Before he knew it he had asked if she would keep him company through the night.

They slept together in his bed. Outside a storm raged, but in his fortress they felt the warmth that comes with sharing the darkness with a person you trust, and in this warm way they soothed each other to sleep. He wanted her to wrap herself around him. He wanted to be held and loved and so she did those things. And afterwards, she watched him sleep, heard his quiet breath, listened to his murmurs as he lay there and her heart filled in a way it never had before.

In the morning Lucido's bravery had disappeared. He pushed Tristessa away, made her leave without saying goodbye. Graceless and clumsy, he made her feel ashamed of a night when they had simply given each other comfort. As he watched her leave, he felt a mix of anger, guilt and relief. He went inside before she was out of sight, banged the door and bolted it firmly as if to keep her out. But she followed him around all day inside his head and for days afterwards. He kept seeing her confused look, the way she walked away from him with a bowed head, little pools of unacknowledged and unwept tears trembling in the bottom lids of her eyes.

PROSPECT

Snow falls outside, and a wind has sprung up. The weather channel predicts six inches of snow this weekend. While you pack your bag you think about practical things like weather and socks. It is a good way to avoid the other, pressing issues. You pack two pairs of shoes.

The Princess is perched on your bed. 'How long will you be gone?'

It's not a question you can answer, so you shrug.

You don't know how cold it gets in San Antonio but you think the nights might be chilly. You pack three sweaters.

'Do you want me to look in on your apartment?'

'Okay.' You pack a handful of underwear, and a pair of pyjamas.

The Princess has picked up your notebook from where it was lying beside the bed. She is turning it over and over in her hands. You want to tell her not to open it. You almost tell her to put it down. She might not understand.

'Aren't you going to ask me about Robert?' she asks,

tracing her finger around the forms of the intertwined lovers on the cover.

'Well, l can probably guess most of it. He was upstairs in your room this morning and the two of you are finishing each other's sentences. It doesn't take an Einstein to figure out ...'

'He's on probation,' she says.

'Oh, for goodness' sake!'

'You don't approve of me, do you?' she asks, surprising you with the directness of the question.

'It's not so much about approval — you know you do things that I would never do.' You pause. 'But it's your life.' And pause again. 'And I do love you.'

She looks at you directly, and she says, 'I love you too.' And something in you swells and is happy.

You pack five blouses. Two of them are white, one pink, one blue, one red.

'What will you do in San Antonio?'

'Family stuff. My aunt's house, I mean, *my* house,' correcting yourself.

You are meeting a man called Ignacio Sanchez, who will take you to your aunt's house, and you will have to make arrangements. Arrangements. You cannot even begin to think what those arrangements might be. You do not want to go. You're doing it because you have to.

'Why didn't you go there before?'

'I just didn't, okay?'

She's looking at you now. She's never seen you like this, so quiet and firm. 'I've never seen you like this,' she says.

'Do you believe in fate?'

'Absolutely, when it comes to love. With everything else, I believe in free will.' She giggles.

'Aubrey says that love is an ideologically suspect construct.' You go into the bathroom to pack your toiletries. Toothbrush, toothpaste.

'And what do you believe, Theney?' she calls out to you.

Soap, lotion. 'Aubrey says he ...' you begin.

The Princess' voice interrupts you. 'When Lucido met Tristessa he was very alone and that was how he wanted it to be. After all, his home was barricaded against the world and the barricades had not been built by accident.'

You drop the toiletries bag, and rush into the bedroom where you try to grab your notebook from her.

But she pushes you away. 'Let me finish! This is good!

'He had dedicated many years to refining the art of chronicling, and had become a master. Like any artist, Lucido knew that the source of the beauty and meaning he could put in his writing was somewhere deep in his heart, somewhere that some people can only see in themselves if life has sent them there with kicks and blows.'

She shuts the journal. 'So,' she says. 'You like him then.'

'Aubrey? Yes. I do. But nothing's happened, and nothing probably will happen ...'

'I ... Robert told me something. Theney, Aubrey has some problems.'

'What do you mean? He seems fine to me — a bit broken and damaged, but he's decent.'

'He's slept with every singer he's ever worked with.'

'Oooh, that's wicked, and it's never happened before in the history of jazz.'

She ignores the sarcasm. 'He gets terribly depressed. Once he tried to take his own life. You should stay away from people like that.'

'Why should I stay away? And what do you mean *"people like that"*?' A little part of you looks out the window at that Nebraska wind making all the trees sway and the snow swirl, and then looks into your heart and sees the Daniel sadness and the half-way-across-the-world-away-from-home-sadness, and feels again the weight of Aubrey's pain, that thing that sits on his heart and stifles him. Perhaps she doesn't understand ... 'Perhaps he has a reason to be depressed. Some things take a long time to pass.'

'It's okay for a little while,' she continues, 'but then a person should move on.'

She doesn't understand.

'It makes me mad,' she says, 'like homeless people and the unemployed. All they need is determination and to get off their butts ...'

'We're going to be late,' you interrupt. 'I need to finish this. Will you be ready in fifteen?'

'I'll go and do my hair and change my sweater. I'll see you in the car, out front of the apartments.' And finally, she leaves.

On the way to the airport, the Princess says wistfully, 'You'll love Texas.'

'Is there anything special I should see?' you ask.

'Well, you should see the Alamo — that's in San Antonio. Have you heard of that?'

You nod, remembering the John Wayne movie.

She continues. 'And you could go to the Hill Country, but it would be better in April when there are Blue Bonnets,' she says. And then asks, 'Why don't you wait till April? You could go to Fiesta. I could come with you.'

Fiesta in San Antonio and you could drive through the Texas Hill Country, in the time of Blue Bonnets. Carpets of them on the hills. You remember Dottie telling you about them. And you saw a poster once, at Dallas Fort Worth airport.

You think out loud. 'Maybe we can go again in April.'

TRISTESSA AND LUCIDO

For all the time that Tristessa had been in this place, she had been in a kind of limbo. And then a thought had begun to form, somewhere in the back of her mind, that somehow in this strange place, with this difficult man and these uncomfortable feelings, her life would move forward into its next phase and that she would find answers to her questions.

Tristessa realised that perhaps she had been right in the beginning when she thought that Lucido might be important. He had brought her back to the world and had opened her heart again, when she hadn't even realised it was closed. By beginning to love Lucido, she was remembering the one thing in life that provides us all with purpose and gives us all strength. This one thing, love, was at the root of her gift as a warrior in the war against demons. That was not all it was. Love was the root of all the good in her life. And meanwhile, no matter what might happen with Lucido, she had lost nothing. She was still a warrior in possession of all the gifts she started with, enriched with a deeper understanding of love. All she had to do now was find a way to make sense of what was happening between her and Lucido and decide what to do about that.

He sometimes seemed to want her, but he said he didn't. He walked through the world with a wound he would not look at. Because of her training and all the skills she had learned from her father and honed over her years wandering the world, she could see Lucido's demons — they were strong and well entrenched. What was she to do?

PROSPECT

As the plane lands at San Antonio airport, the sun is shining and you are caught in the spell that the new day's sun can weave. It frightens you, the feeling that you're here because your fate has brought you here. The idea of fate in Prospect never frightened you, but here something different is going on.

You go to Dottie's house, and stand outside the front gate. It is a beautiful place, with iron lace and dignity, and a garden she lavished with care. It looks like Como House, in Melbourne, with all the grandeur of another era. Behind the house, you can see the trees that line the riverbank. You can imagine growing up here. You hold the key in your hand, the key she gave you when you were nineteen years old and first finding your way in Melbourne. You don't want to use the key. It is not your house. Instead, you want her to open the door and come out. You do not want this to be your house now. You want things to be as they used to be.

And then you think about Aubrey and the owl and the golden tree. Maybe tomorrow you will go inside.

Later, you are in bed at the Holiday Inn, writing in

your book while the people in the room next door party. You had every intention of cleaning up and going out to see and feel the town and maybe dance and drink tequila, but that old thing happens again when you don't want to do it all by yourself. You cannot.

The morning comes, and you wake with your head propped up on pillows and an ink-stain on the sheet where your pen dropped out of your hand and lay for half the night with its top off. You have slept well, despite the party next door and the turmoil inside.

You swim in the hotel pool and remember that waking this way is sometimes the best way. Floating in the coolness of a body of water, then growing legs and walking out to face the day.

But a world weariness sets in as you saunter along the Riverwalk and find a place to break your fast. All the places are just setting up. The waiter who serves you seems bemused by your early presence. Drinking surprisingly decent coffee in the Riverwalk wasteland that will only start to come to life in the afternoon, in a city that still seems to act as though it is Spanish, you decide with uncharacteristic clarity that it is time to stop just living in the wallow of your life, splashing about in the fine mud of what you fear, what you want to be and what is disappointing.

Still, without Dottie in your life, you feel at your loneliest ever. Dottie's absence and the strange things that Aubrey makes you feel have piled on top of each other to make you feel completely isolated.

And meantime, the aloneness is not always comfortable, but it is yours and you can almost convince yourself that you are alone because you choose to be. There is a type of purity in that. And the fact that you never seem to meet that special person, to 'get it right', is no big deal in introspective moments such as this. You can walk around without your dream companion and still believe he will eventually appear on the horizon. You accept it is not Daniel. You are beginning to accept that. But you know that you must feel at least as much as you felt for Daniel before you let a person in again.

And then there's Aubrey. But you still find it hard to think about him, difficult to get your head around what he is, what he's meant to be.

The Princess says there is someone out there for you. And sometimes the feeling that you don't know how much longer you can go on like this sneaks up on you and gives you a scare. You feel helpless in the face of your loneliness, living each day as a goal in itself, because looking beyond is just too hard. You can put your hand on someone else's heart and take away their pain — you cannot do it to your own. And yet you also mostly feel that the well of strength in you will never dry up. You might think you are at the bottom. You might think that you are lifting the last bucket or two of water out of there, and then it will be dry and something in you will die, but that never seems to happen. What scares you just a little is that recently you doubt how long you can go on, and you have been wondering if the well might actually dry up soon.

And so you finish your coffee, filling in time before you have to meet Ignacio Sanchez and face the reality of your aunt's death and what she left you. You take a walk along West Commerce Street, ripe for miracles.

One is delivered to you, in the shape of a girl looking for the Greyhound depot. Aieee, if you know the smell of sadness and despair from your own history, this girl has been bathing in it recently. You see it in her light, and you smell it in the miasma around her. She knows the name of the street she needs to be on, but she can't find it and you have a map. Somehow, between the two of you, you still get lost. But you had needed to meet — her for hope of other choices, you for reminders of the blessings.

'I'm going home to New Hampshire,' she says. 'I was here with my fiancé and he left me high and dry. We're buying a house together. We're going to get married. You know, we spent three thousand dollars last night. Three thousand.'

This surprises you. She doesn't look like someone with access to that much money. God knows what they spent it on ... and she goes on to tell you that somehow last night they ended up in different places and he rings her at two a.m. at the hotel where she waits for him, and asks her to wait.

'Please wait,' he says. 'I'll be there soon.' And she can hear a woman's voice behind him. And the woman is giggling.

But she waits for him. She is his girlfriend and she loves him and she waits. The hotel says she has to check out by eleven a.m. and he still hasn't turned up, so she leaves and now is going home with money wired by her family.

You imagine how that San Antonio night enhanced by whatever three thousand dollars can buy must have felt. And since you were not in it, your imagination fills in the gaps and you see her and her masked fiancé in a bizarre mixture of Venetian Carnevale (that you've seen only in films) and weird torchlight, in some crazed dancing frenzy on the Riverwalk. And even though you think your life has been different and strange, nothing like that has ever happened to you.

She has left her job and her family in New Hampshire. She has nothing here except her love, and the question of a woman giggling in the background, and the deposit on a house not even in her name, and now she's going home, but twenty-one years old. And this heaviness in her heart will now and forever be part of the fabric of her life.

And then you know what you have to say to her, as the two of you round the corner and see the Greyhound depot. You say, 'Well, you know shit happens, and I know that's not the best thing for you to hear right now, but I was just walking along thinking about my own life and it went something like this: *'Why me, why is this shit happening to me?'* So you see you're not alone, you're in good company. My aunt, who lived right here in San Antonio, once told me that we're all just little specks of dust, dancing in a beam of light. She said that when you know that, nothing can hurt you.'

The girl smiles then, which is good to see, and you see that her burden is lighter for having heard what you just said. Your mood lightens considerably too, because what you just said sounds more like something from a comedy than a tragedy and the shit doesn't actually feel like shit any more. Which is how miracles are delivered and how you always find the extra water at the bottom of the well.

You hold her hand as you say goodbye, and you watch her lighten a little more from your touch. But you do not put your hand on her heart. It feels good to share her troubles without taking them away, and your own load seems suddenly less heavy.

At the hotel, you dial the number for Mr Sanchez and when he answers you tell him that you must return to Prospect.

He is surprised. 'But your aunt's house? Did you want to finalise, to make some arrangements?'

The lie comes easy. 'Something urgent has come up. The house will have to wait.

'I'll fly out first thing in the morning. Would you keep looking after things here for me? I'll be back in April. Do you mind?'

He does not mind. For Ignacio Sanchez, this is easy money. You have told him to keep the house clean and take care of the garden, otherwise leaving everything as it is. For this he draws a weekly amount. And you know he uses the house from time to time for family who come to San Antonio to see him. Your aunt trusted him, and you do too. You have neither the will nor the inclination not too. And besides you simply are not ready to take over. Soon … but not yet.

'If there's anything I can do for you …' he says.

'Thanks, but no. I just need to get back.'

The next plane with a seat available is in the morning

so you have to stay another night at the Holiday Inn. And that night Aubrey tries to take his own life again, a thousand miles away in Prospect. Though, of course you did not know that he had done this yet because you are still in Texas and you have not checked your voicemail and heard the message from the Princess.

In Texas you dream of snow — geysers of snow that reach all the way up into the big sky, and wake feeling that the dream is about losing your home, or giving it up. You fly back to Prospect and Linklatters, where you plan to wear a deep red lipstick and laugh under dimmed lights. You have to change planes at St Louis airport and while you wait, you watch people, all in transit, as they walk past you, from one gate lounge to another, filling in time or rushing to catch a flight. You watch their constant movement for nearly two hours. The windows in the concourse are fogged from all their breathing and the moving walkway shudders beneath them and not one of these souls looks happy — or even alive. Set expressions, pale skin, and there's a feel about it of a science-fiction nightmare, as though they are zombies or badly done replicas of humans — missing something vital, some essence of life that would make them real. You try to make your face look alive, so that you do not appear to be one of them. You could not bear to be one of them.

TRISTESSA AND LUCIDO

Lucido thought of himself as an old tired man. But Tristessa thought differently. She did not think Lucido was old and tired. She was not as embittered as he was and where he had lost hope, she looked at him and saw promise and no lies.

It takes many years to destroy hope and in this respect at least, Tristessa was still at the beginning of her life's journey. She thought Lucido was beautiful and gifted and she admired him, no matter how much he told her to stay away. If some of the things he did were hurtful, she looked at them with compassion and kept in mind the essence of the man, which she knew was good. She believed in him, and cared about him, even as he pushed her away with one hand and pulled her to him with the other. It seemed to her that this was a man with a great capacity for love, who had simply forgotten some of love's lessons and how to apply them to his own life. He put love into his chronicles, into all his writing. He had loved his family when they were alive and he still loved their memories. He loved his friends. He had just forgotten how to love himself.

Tristessa saw that Lucido's demons had taught him so well about fear and loss that now he closed himself to any situation that could possibly lead him to experience them again. And when he closed the door on fear and loss, Lucido also closed the door on the potential for joy and fulfillment that comes with someone you trust and love.

Tristessa knew that demons cannot be beaten with force and firepower. They can only be beaten with beauty and integrity, with a pure soul and a good heart, clear eyes and a loud laugh. All these gifts she carried with her. Still, she knew that demons are the cleverest of enemies. They nest in human hearts and feed on fear and anger, and even as they feed on those emotions, they help their host create more.

And so, Tristessa decided that she would fight Lucido's demons. She would place her faith in love and rout the darkness from the places where it rested in his heart. She would use all she had learned in her years as a warrior to give Lucido back a picture of the light.

It seemed to Tristessa that there was only one way for this to end — the light must win against the forces of darkness. Love and courage must win against fear and pain. And we should not forget that since Tristessa was a young warrior, she had not learned to turn her back on such battles without at least trying to shine a light on the darkness — to bring light to those dark spaces in Lucido's heart.

PROSPECT

Linklatters has to wait, since there are three drastic, frantic voicemails from the Princess waiting for you at home, and they tell you that Aubrey has done the unforgivable, and let his demons win. She doesn't say much in the messages, except 'Where are you?' and again 'Where are you?' and 'Aubrey's taken some pills. He's in the hospital.' You listen, not really absorbing, and then the phone is in its cradle and you have grabbed a bottle of gin and half a six-pack of tonic and you are walking out the door to her apartment because you don't know what else to do. What is the protocol when someone you are falling for commits suicide, or attempts it? In your mind you utter a silent prayer, 'God help me let him still be alive, unless he really wanted to go, in which case set him free and let him go and spare me, Father spare me, from too much pain.' You sometimes wonder if God minds that you pray only when things are really bad or really amazing. That the rest of the time it doesn't cross your mind to attempt a dialogue.

You knock and the Princess opens the door and hugs you tight and pulls you inside, relieving you of the bottles only long enough to use them to fill up a glass for you to drink from.

'Oh my God, Theney,' she says 'I don't know what to say.'

'Is he all right?'

And she nods. She nods, and when you see her nod you start to laugh — but it's like the laugh in primary school on Armistice Day when a class of ten-year-olds gets the giggles during the two minute silence of remembrance for people who died when their grandparents were young.

She motions you to the couch and makes you a drink. Between giggles you drink steadily and talk about your trip to San Antonio, and you cannot stop talking and telling stories and, every minute, growing more angry at him for this unexpected change in circumstance. There is a thread of fear in your mind that this was your fault, that it was something you did.

The Princess listens quietly to your babble for a little while, until there is a pause. 'I don't quite know what to say to you,' she says.

'There's nothing to say.'

'I'm very disappointed in Aubrey.'

'Disappointed. That's an interesting word to use.'

'What would you prefer?'

'I don't know, but perhaps something more compassionate. Something that shows you understand.'

'Well, that's just it,' she says. 'I don't understand at all. It's weak, and there's never any excuse for that sort of thing.'

'It's not *"that sort of thing!"*, you say, exasperated. 'It's pain, despair. How did you get to be so ... brittle?'

'Now *that's* an interesting word to use.' She's trying to light the last match from a Linklatters matchbook. The match is old and the matchbook is ragged, so the task is doomed to fail.

You watch her, fascinated. Strike. Strike. Strike. Her movements are short and jerky. Her cigarette hangs from the corner of her mouth. 'Darn,' she keeps saying. 'Darn, darn, darn.' Normally that would crack you up, but here and now you feel anger building inside you. Every time she strikes the match the level of your anger goes up a notch.

'Will you stop it!'

'It's ... my ... last ... match ...' She punctuates the sentence with more attempts at striking. And then she strikes the match angrily one last time and it catches, but the lighted head flies off and lands among the silk and tassled cushions at the end of her sofa.

You jump up and start throwing cushions on to the floor. The Princess pulls her feet up off the floor and backs into a corner of the sofa, a look of horror on her face, her cigarette held high in her hand, as if she is protecting it from something. You can't see the match head anywhere. No smoke, no flames, but you know you have to find it. The throwing of cushions on the floor and the scrambling hunt for the match head have allowed you to act out your anger at her, at Aubrey. They give you some alternative to taking her by the shoulders and shaking her.

In the end you give up. 'I can't find it.'

'It's okay. It's probably gone out by now.'

'Maybe. Do you want me to get some matches from my place?'

'Maybe later.' She giggles and puts the cigarette back in the packet. 'It makes Robert mad when I smoke.'

'What happened to "Bobby"?'

'What do you mean?'

'You used to call him Bobby.'

'He hates that too. If I have to compromise I might as well choose something easy. If he wants me to call him Robert, that's okay, but I'll probably never stop smoking.'

She gets up and goes to the kitchen, puts ice in her glass and fills it. 'More gin?'

'No. Yes. Okay.'

'Well,' she says, handing it to you, 'I guess it's good for you to find out about Aubrey before it was too late.'

'Find what out?'

'Well, you know, how unsuitable he is.'

'All I've found out is that he's in pain. He feels that there's no hope and he's been driven to do something that most people find unthinkable. All I've found out is that he has the capacity to feel things very deeply and that he is in need of help. Just that. He needs to find a way to feel better about life. I'm just grateful he didn't actually kill himself, because I think he's got a lot to offer ...' You falter.

And then she says, 'Let's go out.'

'Okay. I have to change.' You stand, and realise the drink has gone to your head. 'I'm drunk. A bit.'

'That's all right. I'll look after you for a change.'

216

'Sure?'

'Mmmm hmmm. I'll come get you in a bit.'

'Okay.' And you stumble off to your apartment.

TRISTESSA AND LUCIDO

Now that Tristessa had made the decision to fight Lucido's demons, she found that there was another obstacle — she could not reach Lucido. He withdrew completely from sight. She went to all the places where she'd seen him in the past, but he did not appear. Three times, in different weeks, she tried to knock on his door, but it stared silently back at her. She felt sure he was inside, but he would not answer her. She was not completely surprised. When it comes to self-preservation, demons are not stupid.

Weeks passed. Then, one day, Tristessa saw Lucido on the other side of the street and after just a moment's hesitation she crossed the cobblestones to meet him. She was relieved that he smiled when he saw her — she would not have been surprised if he had walked away or ignored her. When she reached him, she held out her hand in a friendly gesture, and said hello.

Lucido surprised her then by taking her hand and holding it and asking her: 'Will you come to my house tomorrow?' He looked sideways at her, and seemed a little nervous. 'I have something to show you.' He turned away and left her standing in the middle of the market, not sure what to think. He seemed lighter than when she had last seen him, and happier. Perhaps he had found a way to fight his own battle against darkness.

She smiled to think that this might be true. Like most warriors, she knew that the demons inside a person are best vanquished by their host. It is a surer way of permanent banishment than if they are vanquished by another.

PROSPECT

Who says that alcohol numbs your perceptions? Just enough can strip away protection you've spent months building up. Two glasses of gin can put you there — in a reality with no soft focus.

The front door of your apartment still scares you a little. Not the door itself, which is relatively harmless, made as it is of wood with a peephole and a double deadlock and chain. It's what you see when you step inside the door, and what that does to you. When you open the front door, you are entering a world where you are alone, and self-sufficient. A solitary world. There were times, not so long ago, when you were still in gin-and-tonic mode, that you would open up the door and hesitate just long enough to throw your work bag inside then leave and head to Linklatters for the evening. And when you came back at half past ten or eleven you were so tired and full of alcohol that you could make it all the way inside the door and to bed without that wave of sadness and aloneness threatening to drown you.

That memory hits you now, with two drinks inside you and the news about Aubrey that you still haven't processed. You step inside the door and close it behind you, but it is impossible to step further inside the apartment. A great weight presses you down and you slump to your knees on the floorboards, then lie down and curl up with your knees under your chin and your cheek resting on your hands. You lie there with your eyes open, not moving, looking at the floorboards in front of your face. They could do with a sweep. There are dust bunnies everywhere. The Princess will be here soon ... You should get up. You should ... The phone rings and you jump up, banging your head on the door handle.

'Shit!'

A scramble for the phone and you hear the most amazing sound.

'Hello?' you hear. 'Hello?'

'Aubrey! I ... How are you? ... I just heard ... How ...?'

'I'm ... Well, I'm alive,' his laugh is bitter. 'And now my doctor thinks I need a shrink. He says it was a "cry for help". I told him that was crap. I wanted to do it and I'm pissed it didn't work.'

'Why didn't it work?'

He sighs. 'Lloyd dropped by, as it happens. I'd forgotten that he said he was going to. He still had a key from the last time I went away when he was going to water the plants. He had no business coming inside. He normally doesn't. I'm not talking to him at the moment.'

'I'm glad you called. I wasn't sure if I should. Are you at home?'

'Yes, I am. They let me back home this afternoon and I had to make all sorts of ridiculous promises. Look I won't keep you; but I just wanted to say that you mustn't let — what do you call her? — the Princess? You mustn't let her give you any weird ideas. None of this has anything to do with you. You know, I understand completely. She told me … well,' he laughs again, a little nervous. 'I was pretty drunk …' He pauses.

You open your mouth and nothing comes out.

'Hello?' he says. 'Hello?'

'It's okay,' you say. 'I hadn't heard a thing about your conversation with her. You can rest easy.'

'You hadn't heard a thing? I thought you girls told each other everything. At least, that's what she said.'

'That's not exactly true. And besides, she hasn't had a chance. I only just got home.' Through your front window, you see movement outside. It is the Princess, walking up the steps to your door. 'I have to go. There's someone at the door. Can I call you later?'

'I guess,' he says. 'Though I can't guarantee I'll answer. I'm feeling anti-social tonight.'

'Is someone with you?'

'No, and don't you start. Everybody thinks they have to watch me twenty-four seven at the moment. It's just plain ridiculous.'

The Princess knocks.

'Sorry. I'm just worried. I guess everybody will be for a while. But I'll definitely call you later, okay? Bye.'

'Bye,' he says. You hang up, and open the door.

'Who was that,' she wants to know.

'Just someone from work.'

She looks at you. 'Oh, really?' and she smiles as though she knows.

'I'm sorry, but I haven't even started getting ready.'

'That's okay. Can I call Robert from here? He might be able to meet up with us later.'

'Sure,' you say. 'I'll just be a minute. Come up when you're done.'

TRISTESSA AND LUCIDO

Tristessa was at Lucido's fortress early and she hesitated outside the door, calming herself before knocking firmly on the solid door. She had butterflies in her belly that she wished she didn't feel. In all her years of fighting she had rarely felt a moment's nervousness and the sensation was unsettling.

Lucido answered the door, took her hand, pulled her inside and led her in silence to a closed door at the end of a long hallway. He paused and then turned towards her, taking both her hands in his. 'Since my family died, I have lived a very quiet life,' he said. 'My heart is dead and that is not your fault. I will not ask your forgiveness for last time we met since even if you gave me that gift, you would not know half the things you are forgiving me for.'

He stopped and turned away — as though uncomfortable with his own words — before opening the door, leading her through the doorway, and up a hundred steps. She watched his strong back as she followed and wondered how he could think of himself as old and weak; he walked steadily with no shortness of breath up the steps towards whatever it was he needed to show her.

When they reached the top they faced yet another closed door and he said, 'Close your eyes Tristessa.' And when she did, he opened the door and walked her through before dropping her hand. She stood, eyes closed, and felt warmth on her eyelids, and smelt spring flowers. 'Open them now,' said Lucido, and when she did, Tristessa looked around her in wonder. She was in the middle of a room filled with sunshine. The walls were yellow and hung with beautiful pictures and tapestries. Warm rugs were scattered around the floor. The windows, which covered the entire south wall, were open to the streaming sunlight and the warm breeze brought the scent of spring flowers into the room from the window boxes that hung outside. The room was a striking contrast to the cold darkness of the rooms downstairs.

Tristessa turned to Lucido with a question in her eyes, but he put his finger to his lips, gesturing her to silence. 'This room has been closed since my family died,' he said, 'and now it is open again, and I wanted you to see. That is all.' And with that, he moved back across the room and opened the door, indicating that she should go, which she did, step by step, down a hundred steps until she was back in the darkened room below.

She turned to him and was silent for a moment. Finally she spoke. 'I must leave … .Thank you.' And she ran out the door and into the street.

PROSPECT

It is not until you are settled at the bar at Linklatters that you broach the subject with her. 'What did you do while I was away?'

'Oh,' she says, 'nothing special.' A drag on her cigarette. 'Though I did run into Aubrey here the night you left.'

'Did you talk to him?'

'Of course.'

'And?'

'Well,' she's drinking vodka and tonic tonight and she swirls the ice around with her straw while thinking what to say. 'Well, we had a nice talk. That's all.'

'And did I come into it?' Your brain, affected by alcohol, is having trouble holding onto these threads of conversation. 'Did he talk about me at all?'

'I'd rather not talk about it, given recent events. I think what's happened speaks for itself.'

You're a bit slow sometimes. The Princess isn't. She can make the best of any situation, and get the upper hand without even trying. She dangles information in front of you and then withholds it. It drives you crazy whenever she does that.

One of the biggest differences between the two of you has to do with her speed and your depth. Still waters run deep. Deep waters run slow. And she's a bubbling stream — a laughing shining golden rush of water over glistening pebbles in a summer creekbed.

Before you can even begin to say any of the angry words she prompts with her games, she's had a drink bought for her by the man across the bar. You get a drink as well, but it's her he wants and that game is obviously more fun than the one she's been playing with you. She looks across at him with a smile and he raises his glass to her, and barely acknowledges you. That's okay. Thank goodness he doesn't have a mate looking for leftovers. She has a boyfriend but it doesn't stop her. Some things never stop.

She hasn't forgotten you, though. 'It's probably better if you don't know,' she says.

'Why? That just tells me that what was said was important enough to hold back.'

'I don't want to hurt you.'

'The only way you'll hurt me is to hold back on the truth. All I want is the truth. Whether you think it means anything or not. Whether it hurts me or not. At least I know where I stand if I have the truth.' She doesn't look convinced. 'Look,' you continue, 'if I had a terrible disease and the doctor had told my family that I had only six months to live, but they decided not to tell me because they didn't want to upset me ... Would you tell me?'

'That wouldn't happen.'

'It could. And maybe it's an extreme example, but ...' You pause. 'If you were a real friend you would tell me.'

'Okay, okay! I'll tell you. But if you get upset ...'

'Just ...' This is ridiculous. It's probably nothing, you think to yourself.

'He said he was growing rather fond of you ...'

A great sigh of relief washes over you. But she is not finished.

'I told him you were in San Antonio with a man.'

You put your glass down and turn towards her. 'What?!'

'Well,' she says, swirling her ice casually and taking a sip. 'He needed to know that you're in demand. You don't want to make it too easy for them, you know. That way they don't respect you. They need to know they have to fight for you. I was only trying to help. You know, it does them good to hear ...'

'You ... I can't believe ... Fuck!' You put a five dollar bill under your glass. 'I'm going.'

She tinkles laughter after you. 'Lighten up! It's nothing! Trust me, I know what I'm talking about!' As you open the door to Linklatters and head into the cold night, she's still calling after you.

'Theney? Theney?'

Under your breath, you mutter, 'Piss off!' It's been a long time since you were this angry. You go to the supermarket up the road from his house. It has a payphone and you call his number and it is busy so you decide to hell with it and drive there. The door downstairs is — thank God — propped open and you run up to his front door and you knock. He doesn't answer. You knock again. And knock again. You know he's in there. The phone was busy. Unless ... He couldn't have, could he? He said he wouldn't do it again. Or did he? You try to go through the conversation in your mind, and cannot remember anything except his 'Hello? Hello?' and how happy that made you. You imagine him in his bath, surrounded by blood. You imagine him senseless on the floor with spittle on the corners of his mouth.

You go up the street again, this time up the other way. You've seen a phone up there before that you can use from your car. But in the end you're shaking so much you can't line the car up properly, so you stand there on McAllister Street, outside a gas station, at yet another payphone, crying your eyes out, the droplets freezing on your cheeks. You call Lloyd. What else are you supposed to do?

'Lloyd,' you sob. 'I think ... Aubrey isn't answering! He won't open his door. Should I call 911? What should I do?'

'Where are you?'

'Just up the street from his place. On that phone outside the gas station on McAllister.'

'I'll meet you at his place,' he says. 'Don't worry. I still have a key.'

You have a couple of quarters left. You have a terrible feeling in your gut. Just one more time, and please God let him answer. You dial and the phone rings. It rings then goes to the answering machine.

'This is Aubrey. Leave a message.'

'Aubrey, this is Theney ... pick up if you can. Aubrey, please ...' Nothing.

You get into your car and drive to the apartment. Lloyd arrives and knocks but there's no answer. He yells out, 'Aubrey, I'm coming in. I have a key.' He unlocks the door and the two of you go inside. He is not there. You both check every corner.

'Did you see if his car was there?'

'No,' you admit.

'Well, come on, before he comes home and finds us here.'

Lloyd takes your arm and steers you outside. Aubrey's car is not in the street. 'Tell me everything that happened. Tell me why you were so worried.'

You tell him and he reassures you. 'He won't try it again. Rosa seems sure, and I always trust her judgement on things like this. She says the moment has passed. You met Rosa, didn't you? Look, he must be out. If someone else was calling at the exact same time as you were, and leaving a message on the machine, then the line would be busy. It's happened to me before. Come back to Linklatters and I'll buy you a drink.' And when he sees you hesitate. 'The Princess left with Robert a few minutes ago. It's okay. You'll be all right. Come on.'

TRISTESSA AND LUCIDO

As it is with humans, so it is with demons. Lucido's demons had been confident of continuity. They had not figured on the arrival of a young warrior with a good heart. They had not expected that Lucido would remember his long-forgotten courage. They had not imagined he would start to heal his pain by re-opening a warm room at the top of a hundred stairs, filled with sunshine and the smell of spring flowers. And so began a time of great conflict within the re-awakening heart of Lucido and of great efforts on the part of demons to keep the darkness dark and keep Lucido's fear alive.

Once again Lucido and Tristessa did not speak for some weeks. Lucido had found a new well of artistic energy inside him, and he was also reaching out from his dark world to renew acquaintanceships with those who had long ago given him up for dead. He felt revitalised. Every now and then Tristessa would come into his thoughts and he would think that he should talk to her, and be her friend, but whenever the thought crossed his mind, he would suddenly find he needed to drink another pint of ale or distract himself with some of his new friends, or fill another page with golden words.

In between times, like the quiet moments after lying down

and before falling asleep, he would feel a kind of pain like searing emptiness. He would go to sleep eventually, and then he would forget. When he slept, his dreams were fields of conflict and on many mornings when he woke he felt more tired than the night before. Yet, when he was awake, he filled as many moments as he could with action and colour and laughter and it seemed to him that he was doing well. He was not really happy, and he sensed that something was missing, but for the most part everything seemed to be tolerable.

PROSPECT

Linklatters is warm and the lights are dimmed with not many customers tonight. A haven. You take out your notebook and look at the cover. Lloyd pours you a Shiraz and sees that you want to be left alone.

'Let me know if you need anything,' he says.

You smile at him and touch his sleeve as he turns away. 'Lloyd, thanks. Thank you. I mean it.'

'I know you do, doll.' He winks and walks away.

A few pages later, he's back. 'Last drinks,' he says. 'You want a last one, Theney?'

'Okay, why not.'

You've drunk the last of the bottle so he has to open a new one. 'Same again?'

You nod and watch him pour. 'You seem to be thinking,' you observe.

He doesn't answer immediately. 'I have a message from Rosa. My Rosa,' he says eventually. 'You remember her, don't you? She was at Aubrey's party.'

Yeah, you remember. You remember Leonard Cohen.

'She does readings. With Tarot cards. She doesn't talk about it much, and she doesn't really do readings any more but … She wants to do a reading for you — if you're interested. She asked me to ask next time I saw you.'

'It's all right, thanks anyway. I don't generally indulge.'

'Well, that's okay. She did say you probably wouldn't.' He pauses. 'I'm not sure what this means, but she said to tell you that she knows about the owl and the golden tree.'

TRISTESSA AND LUCIDO

Tristessa, too, felt energised, but she also knew that something was not right. She tried to see Lucido, but he avoided her and even when he had no choice but to talk to her, their conversations were shallow and unsatisfying. She wondered what to do, but had no answers. Perhaps it was time to leave the city and return to her warrior life. Perhaps she should return to her village. But somehow she could not bring herself to leave. It was as though something remained undone, and she could not leave until completely satisfied that she had fulfilled her obligation.

Spring turned to summer, then autumn and winter. One night when the first snow of the season was falling, Tristessa found herself walking past a tavern where Lucido had just completed a reading of his recent work. From the window, she saw him and decided to go in and say hello. She walked in and moved towards the table where he sat with a group of people. And then she saw that he had his arm around the waist of the woman beside him. Tristessa saw him lean towards her. She saw him whisper in the woman's ear then kiss her lips and laugh softly. The woman saw Tristessa watching. A smile flickered triumphantly across her face, and Tristessa felt the room begin to spin. She knew she had to get away, although her legs would not move. When she could rouse herself, Tristessa half ran, half stumbled out the door into the snow, where she leaned against a post for a moment. All she wanted to do was leave that place and never come back. A hot flush spread from her throat to her face.

Tristessa had experienced many dangers as a warrior. She had fought many types of battles and won. There were few demon encounters in which Tristessa had been defeated — and yet she had never felt this.

PROSPECT

It is two-thirteen in the morning when you sit straight upright in bed. Something is terribly wrong. You swing your legs over the side of the bed and smell the smoke. Jeans, boots, long-sleeved shirt — grabbing these items is almost a reflex. Some remnant from endless summers of living in bushfire-prone Australian bushland has kicked in.

Downstairs the smoke is heavier. You see that it is heaviest around the vent above your bookshelf. The wall is the adjoining one between your loungeroom and hers. The Princess! The Princess is on fire!

You have no fire blanket or fire extinguisher. So you continue with your reflex actions, grabbing a woollen blanket from the linen closet and a bucket from under the sink. In seconds you are next door. She has left her door unlocked again and for once it is a blessing.

Her sofa is on fire. One corner of it at least. And it is less a fire than a smouldering smoky mess. You cannot even see flames, just a pall of smoke in the room and most of it coming from the blackened end of the sofa. A bucket of water and the fire is out.

'What would I do without you, Theney?' The Princess has come down from her bed upstairs and is wrapped in a blanket, watching you.

'Hi. This should be all right now. It must have been that match head. Probably sat there smouldering away all day. I'll leave you to it.' You do not want to have a conversation. You want to get away.

'Theney?'

You turn to look at her.

'I'm sorry. I just care about you. Those things I said … I just want you to be happy.'

'Okay.'

'Theney?'

It seems that you're supposed to say something else. All that comes out is, 'We're very different.'

'Not so different.'

'Very different.'

'Perhaps that's why we're friends.'

'Are we friends?' You turn to face her completely. 'Are we really friends? When we go out, I feel like I'm some sort of chaperone. There are all these little games we play. You do things …'

'What do you mean?'

'You do things I would never do to you. If we're going to be friends I have to be able to trust you.'

'Not necessarily.'

'Yes, necessarily!'

'No. You need to know *how much* you can trust me. And I really am sorry.'

'What do you mean "how much I can trust you"?'

'Well, when we go out, can you trust me to be sensible?'

You shake your head, laughing, despite yourself. 'No!'

'Can you trust me to be here when you need me?'

You look at her carefully. 'I guess.'

'You know who I am, better than most. You know when you can rely on me, and how I'll behave in different situations.' She searches your face.

You don't want to have this conversation. 'Well, I have to get back to bed,' you say.

'Okay. I understand.' And as you walk out the door, she says, 'Don't forget the other part of this.'

'What other part?'

'You need to know when to trust me. But I need to know you won't judge me for being who I am. I am who I am. I might not live a life you understand, but I don't want your life either. It would drive me crazy.'

'I ...'

'And I didn't ... wouldn't ... hurt you on purpose.' She is holding her head up and staring you in the eye, but her eyes are wet.

She's right.

'I love you, Theney. I don't know what I'd do without our friendship.'

Which of course makes you cry. She knows all the right words to say. She understands your buttons.

'Do you want some cocoa?'

You nod. She reaches out her hand and takes yours. 'Come on. We'll make cocoa and sit up in bed and drink it.' She giggles. 'Seeing as some mad Aussie woman turned my sofa into a swimming pool.'

TRISTESSA AND LUCIDO

Tristessa thought about what was happening, and again she felt lost and overwhelmed. One thing that Tristessa had learned well before coming to this city, and from her experiences here — and especially what she had learned from Lucido — was that the battle is not always straightforward even for a warrior who has a good heart, skill and courage. We are all tested constantly by our own demons, and the more fierce the warrior, the greater the test.

One night Tristessa went to sleep and dreamed. When she awoke, she knew with a certainty that when she had opened her heart to Lucido and had decided to fight his demons, she had not been watchful enough — she had somehow let some of the evil creatures into her own life. The pain she felt when she had seen Lucido kiss the other woman was surely evidence that she had demons nestling in her own heart. And so Tristessa set to work to drive them away.

First, Tristessa had to understand the nature of her demons. That part seemed easy enough. She started by listing her fears and she was surprised at how big the list had grown. She set to work to banish them, but there was something bigger than demons that stood in the way of her peace of mind. Something much more confusing.

Tristessa had thought that the previous months of time spent with Lucido had been full of difficult lessons — drawn to him, yet pushed away and, while growing more sure of her own purpose in life, she still thought that she had an obligation to help Lucido find the light in his life again.

But now she was discovering that there was something else. For a number of days after she saw Lucido kiss the woman, people asked her if she felt unwell. She was beset by nausea from when she woke to when she fell into an exhausted sleep for a few hours each night. It was not so much the act of kissing the woman that disturbed her. What hurt and confused Tristessa was the surprise that she had fallen in love with Lucido.

Those who saw Tristessa's surprise were themselves surprised that one so knowledgeable about the use of love in the war against demons could be so blind to her own experience of love.

PROSPECT

Of course you go to meet Rosa. You call first, clutching the napkin on which Lloyd had written the number. She has a nice voice. Warm.

'I'm glad you called. When can you come? Can you come this afternoon?'

'I could, yes.' You wonder if you sound as hesitant as you feel.

'That is good,' she says. 'Before you lose your nerve.'

She and Lloyd live fifteen minutes' drive away, in an old house in an old part of town. You drive past it first, so you know which one it is and then just around the corner you stop your car and sit for a moment, deciding whether to go in. If you do, it will be against your better judgement.

You step out of the car and wrap your coat around you. The winter is beginning to ease. There are still months of snow and slush before spring, but today it feels as though the weight of the season is lifting. The sun today is bright and although the wind is bringing the outside temperature down to a figure you don't even want to think about, there is a stirring. It lightens your step as you walk to the front door of Lloyd's and Rosa's house.

Rosa is as warm as you remembered. She smiles and holds out her hand, grips yours firmly, and looks into your eyes.

'I'm glad you came,' she says. 'Come into my room. I'm making some herbal tea. Do you want some?'

'Yes, thanks.' You follow her into a room where candles burn and the air is filled with clean floral aromas.

'Sit wherever you like. I'll be back in a minute with the tea.'

The chairs are all the same but you pick one that faces the door. It's comfortable, and despite yourself you begin to relax. You see that Lloyd and Rosa are blessed to have each other. The things Lloyd makes you feel at Linklatters, as though you are at home and safe, are the same things you feel in his home, with Rosa. She comes back with the tea.

'Okay, let's begin,' she says, putting a small table in the space between, then sitting across from you. She sits forward and touches your arm. 'I'm so glad you came. Have you ever had a reading done before?'

'Yes, but …'

'Okay, that's okay. I understand.'

She leans back a little and takes a sip of her tea. You do the same.

'Theney, the world's full of people with something extra — some additional ability to see or feel. This is something you need to know. You're not alone.

'And I know this because of my gift. This extra sight has many variations. My gift is that I can see the gift in

others, and I have very clear vision. So any scrap of something extra in a person, and I can spot it. And using the
cards to help me, I can read a person's state, where
they're at in their life.'

You must have let your fear show.

'No, no, no,' she says. I can't read your mind. I don't
intrude. But with the cards I can articulate the things
you already know, even if you don't know you know.'
She takes another sip. 'Let me explain. Everybody knows,
somewhere deep inside them, what they are here to find
out, who they really are, what their dream is, and how
to fulfil it. Everybody. Without exception. You also know
everything you have ever seen, and you know everywhere
you have ever been. You have forgotten nothing.

'I have a theory about my particular abilities. I think
that everybody communicates who they are and what
they want, all the time, at some level. Speech and even
body language are only the most obvious type of articu-
lation. There are other, more subtle, messages being sent
out all the time. Those are the ones that I pick up on,
with the help of the cards.'

She reaches to the table beside her chair and picks
up a deck of cards. 'I think that all the cards do is to
create a by-pass so I can hear what you are unable to say
for yourself. So when we work with the cards, I am speaking to you from your unconscious mind. Making sense
so far?' she smiles.

'So you don't read the future then?'

'No, just the present. Who you are. Where you are.
Where you really are, not just where you think you are.'

'What do I have to do? How does it ...?'

She gives you the cards. 'Here. Shuffle. For as long as you like. Just let your mind relax. Close your eyes if you want to.'

You take the cards. They are bigger than playing cards and harder to handle. You touch them and try to slow your breathing. Something tells you to hold them against your heart with your right hand, which you do. And then you take them in both hands and you shuffle them, slowly. You try to empty your mind, with limited success. As you shuffle, shuffle, shuffle, thoughts float through your mind. You think about the Princess, and your friendship with her. You think about Aubrey and the golden tree; about the goddess Athena and the owl; and about seeing Aubrey stumbling across the snow with a woman on each arm. You think about Dottie and her house in San Antonio, and about Lloyd and the way he pours your wine. You think about when he told Aubrey you were an angel. You think about angels. You think about Daniel, and stop shuffling as you realise that you have let Daniel go.

You start shuffling again, with your eyes still closed. You think about Rosie and her broken arm. You think about your mother in the kitchen at the farm and your father mending fences in the back paddock. A tear tickles the side of your nose and you open your eyes and stop shuffling, tapping the edges of the pack of cards on the table to tidy it. Rosa is smiling at you.

'Good,' she says softly. 'Well done. Cut the cards.'

You pick up the top few cards, splitting the pack.

She starts to deal the cards out, laying them out on the table. And then she speaks. 'So much,' she begins, 'has happened to you to bring you here.' She looks at you. 'You felt called, and you were right. You were called. You have a gift. A healing gift. It scares you. You feel isolated. You feel terribly alone.'

You are transfixed.

'You'll find a way of speaking what you know,' she says. 'You have already started, with this writing you are doing.' She looks at the cards with her head on one side and holds her hand above this one, then that one, for the moment.

'It is a great gift, Theney.' She looks at you. 'You have a great gift. It doesn't have to be such a burden, you know. You feel as though you are in a lonely place. But we are all around you. All you have to do is find your own kind. Find your own way.' She reminds you of Dottie and a wave of sadness washes through you like a sob.

She sits back in her chair. 'Lloyd has a gift, don't you think? Have you ever seen a better bartender? He has a subtle sixth sense that all the best bartenders have. Do you hear anybody talking as though bartenders are anything special? Yet, the best ones are truly gifted. Teachers are the same. Often those with special gifts are drawn to teaching. They don't know why, but they know they have something to offer — something to say, or to give. Your gift is that you can heal some types of pain. But you have already learned the truth of that, I suppose.'

'It never lasts. I can touch someone's heart and take their pain away, and then they make more. And I always mess it up.' You've not been able to talk like this since Dottie died.

'Theney, be good to yourself.' Her voice is gentle.

'You are your own harshest critic.' And then she says, 'You're almost there. You understand the past. You're trying to be in the present. Whatever you are writing, now, keep doing it until it's finished. Within those words you will find the key.' She pauses. 'Do you have any questions?'

'No ... Yes ... No ...'

She smiles at you. 'Which is it?'

You try again. 'Aubrey?'

'You already know that one. You don't need me at all.'

'Is he all right ...?'

'He will be. He needs to remember what he is. What else is music but a different way of expressing a human understanding of the world? His music is how he will make sense of things.

'What are the pictures that move you or the books that inspire you, the songs that swell your heart? Aren't they the ones that show you another way? There's a collage that Aubrey did — it's hanging in his bedroom. Have you seen it?'

You nod.

'Theney, that middle picture is a self-portrait. He took it himself after his wife died, and then placed it right in the centre of all those happy family photographs. What's he saying? He knows, but he doesn't know he knows.'

You remember the cackling toothless hag at the bottle shop. *He knows, but he doesn't know he knows.*

' ... and I don't have a clue,' you finish the thought, surprising yourself.

'Sometimes the greatest gift, Theney, is to truly love

247

another person. And anyone who can do that is gifted. People talk about love as though it's their right. And for sure, love is everybody's birthright. But I'm not talking about the sort of love that lives in romance novels, Theney. Real love is a conscious act. And not many people who say "I love you" really do. That might sound hard, but I believe it to be true. Love's not always easy, and it's not always about romance.'

'Romantic love is an ideologically suspect construct,' you say, remembering.

'Where did you hear that?' she asks.

'Aubrey.'

'Well, whoever said that has been hurt. Look, sometimes the ability to love and live with who a person really is means more than the ability to put your hand on their heart and draw their pain away. Right now, you have the ability to do both. Some gifts come and go, but you will always have the capacity to love. That is a gift you must never forget how to use. It's the most important one.'

You sit back in your chair, looking at her. 'You are telling me something, but it is as though I am hearing it through a fog. I almost understand,' you say. 'Almost.'

'It's okay, Theney. Remember what I said about being easy on yourself. Now's as good a time to start as any.'

'What am I supposed to do?'

She stands. 'You'll figure it out. You're already doing it.'

You stand as well, and you put your hand out. 'Thank you. I think.'

'No, Theney,' she says. 'Thank you. Make sure you come back soon and see me. I want to get to know you.'

She pulls you into a hug, then pushes you away. 'Go on now. Go and do what you have to do.'

TRISTESSA AND LUCIDO

It is default human nature to believe ourselves the root of the problems in our lives and the lives of those we touch, and that is how Tristessa now began to feel. Above all, she felt ashamed of her naïve belief in her own strength and for the way she had become so attached without even realising it. She felt uncertain of her ability to be a good warrior. She wondered if she had ever been a good warrior. She felt foolish for having thought that she should fight Lucido's demons, when in fact he did not want or need her help. He did not want or need her in any way. A multitude of negative thoughts filled her every waking moment. It was a very bad week that seemed to extend forever. But it did end.

The following weekend, as a celebration of the winter solstice, there was to be a gathering of artists, writers and musicians and Tristessa's kind old landlady invited her to come along.

'It is good to reflect,' she said, 'but sometimes reflection for the wrong reasons is destructive. Come out with me and celebrate the solstice. A celebration of the earth's cycle may be just what you need to remind you of the world's gifts.'

Tristessa did not want to go, but could not bear to stay at home with her negative thoughts, so she accepted the artist's invitation.

When they arrived and she had helped the old woman with her coat, she looked around and saw that Lucido was there. She had not known he would be and she had not come prepared.

Tristessa had nothing to say to Lucido, but she was also fearful that she would open her mouth and tell him something she would regret later. She stayed awhile, determined to leave as soon as possible. Before leaving, she plucked up the courage to sit beside Lucido and ask him how he was, hiding from him the things she had discovered since she had seen him kiss the woman in the tavern.

Lucido was happy to see her and in a natural and easy way they began to talk and laugh, and soon it felt to Tristessa as though nothing bad had happened between them. It was almost as it had been when they first met, before either of them had become confused or angry.

As she sat beside him and enjoyed his company, Tristessa realised that the hardest part about being in the same room as Lucido was when she was leaving it, or getting ready to arrive. When she was with him, she felt a peace wash over her, a sense of homecoming. She was beginning to understand how she felt, and what she should do about it. But for the moment, Tristessa gave herself the gift of living in the moment with Lucido.

The celebration was drawing to a close. The music stopped and people began to leave.

'Come outside,' said Lucido. And she followed him out to the back courtyard, wondering what he wanted.

He looked at her and said, 'I understand that you want to save me. But you know I hate to be touched.'

Tristessa said to him, 'I never intended to hurt you.'

'I understand,' he said. 'But it doesn't change the facts. I cannot break down those walls for you. You have to let me make my own mistakes. These are my demons and I must be the one to decide if I will live with them or banish them.'

She accepted what he said. He was speaking clearly and firmly, and she felt she had no right to try to change his mind. The fact that she was in love with him was irrelevant. He did not want her help, and he surely did not want her love. The young warrior tasted defeat, and it was a bitter taste.

PROSPECT

You remember the way to the bench and the golden tree with no trouble at all. The tree is still there, and is still golden, and you are tempted for a moment to go and see what makes it like that. But you change your mind, remembering what Aubrey said. *It's not about knowledge. A rational explanation would destroy it. This way I can believe what I want, and it's true.'*

The feather is still in the back of the bench where you left it, a little the worse for wear. You pick it up and smooth it between your thumb and forefinger, lining up the jagged edges, feeling the smooth curve of it and imagining again the bird it came from. Remembering, too, the yellow eyes of the owl in the cage, lidding and unlidding, saying something to you that you could almost understand. *'Hail Friend.'*

The bench still looks incongruous on its concrete plinth, but you sit on it anyway, pulling your coat tightly around you as protection from the wind. You sit and look at the tree, as you did with Aubrey, trying to capture that afternoon again. What was it? What really happened? As you look, you see that something about the golden tree is different. Something you can't quite touch has definitely changed. You close your eyes, tired at the thought of all that has passed. Wishing an answer were easy. Knowing the ones worth discovering never are.

The wind drops and for a moment the sun is warm on your face. The buzz of freeway traffic reaches your ears intermittently across the wide river flats. In the winter sun, with your eyes closed, you pull your coat around you tight again, but this time it is more a hug than protection against the wind.

Something makes you open your eyes. A golden leaf detaches itself from Aubrey's tree and is fluttering slowly towards the ground. A perfect breathless moment later it disappears. It doesn't touch the ground, but somehow is gone. Perhaps you are more tired than you imagined. But before you can close your eyes, another one begins to fall, and another, and then another, and the tree becomes a cascading waterfall of gold as all its leaves fall. A small dark shape now separates itself from the tree and flies towards you swiftly and smoothly with slow flaps of its wings. A falcon perhaps, or a sparrowhawk, hunting for any tidbits that may have ventured into the warm sunshine.

Your hands, twisting the owl feather, stop suddenly and you hold your breath as the bird lands on a branch of the tree beside you at eye level, almost close enough to touch — not a falcon or a sparrowhawk but an owl. It shuffles for a moment, finding a comfortable perch, then pulls its head into its neck and sits facing you, blinking slowly in the light.

You turn to face the tree again. Now the leaves are

falling faster, a cascade of shimmering gold from the tree, faster and faster. The leaves seem to glow, full of golden light. Beside you, the owl continues to watch you. It seems to be gauging your reaction, looking for a sign that you understand.

In a space of time that could have been a minute or forever, the golden tree becomes just another sleeping tree waiting for spring. You slip the feather in your breast pocket and do up all the buttons on your coat, then leave, not looking back at all.

TRISTESSA AND LUCIDO

In the days that followed, Tristessa decided that she must move on, and leave this man to his demons. You would think that since she loved him, and we know she did, that she would have tried harder to stay and to save him. You might think that, loving him, she would not be able to turn her back. But that was not how it was at all. He had told her that he wanted her to go away, that he could not let her into his heart. She believed she had to leave.

Tristessa made arrangements to return to her village. She wanted to see her father again, and to work beside him. She wanted the peace of simple village life, the acceptance of people who knew and loved her.

The month before she left was a month of mixed feelings. Saying goodbye was harder than she had imagined. As the day of her departure grew closer she realised that in many ways her life here had been richer than any life she had lived in any other place. She realised that her heart would stay behind her when she left, at least for a little while. She remembered that at other times in her life she had become attached to places where she had learned something — even when the lessons had not been pleasant. Do lessons, she wondered, tie you somehow to the place where you did the learning?

PROSPECT

San Antonio shimmers like gold as your plane lands in the early morning light and as soon as you have your luggage, you make your way to the river and to the house.

Mr Sanchez is waiting for you outside the front door. 'It is good to see you again,' he says and you shake his hand, feeling that this, at last, is right and how it should be.

'Sometimes these things take a while,' he says. 'Your aunt, she knew. She said I should not be in a hurry.' He laughs, showing you a gold tooth. 'But it is good that you are here. I am happy for you. Happy to see you.'

You put your suitcase down and take the key out of the side pocket of your handbag where you have been checking every five minutes since you left Prospect to make sure it is still there. The key slides into the lock, and turns easily. You push the door open and walk inside. As you stand in her front hallway — in *your* front hallway — you feel a great sense of peace wash through you and you take a deep, deep breath. A shaft of light through the feature stained-glass window at the top of the stairs shines down onto the mosaic tiles at your feet. As you stand with your arms slowly rising from your sides you look up and realise that the motes of dust swirling and dancing in the golden beams of sunlight you disturbed by walking in the front door are part of the answer to the puzzle you have been walking around with in your heart.

'Welcome home,' says Mr Sanchez.

TRISTESSA AND LUCIDO

Tristessa was learning that everything has its season, and that our own desires rarely turn the earth on its axis, though sometimes it seems like they can. If we are in tune with the universe, it seems as though our wishes make things happen. But that is only because we are in tune and they are the right wishes for us to have at the time. When we are not in tune and wish for things that are not in season, the universe continues resolutely in its own direction, unaffected completely by what it is we think is so important.

Tristessa prepared herself, braced herself internally, for the day when she would leave this place. And meanwhile, when Lucido wanted to spend time with her, she breathed in the moments in the same way as you breathe in the smell of a newly mown hayfield, or the cool clear air at the bottom of a forested valley, or the smell of a baby's neck. She tried to bring things to a close in her mind. After all, Tristessa's home country was half a world away.

As much as she tried, Tristessa was not entirely successful in her efforts to close the doors to her longing.

Lucido turned to her the day before she planned to leave the city and asked her, 'What will happen when you leave?'

She had no answer for him. And Tristessa turned and walked away from Lucido, hearing, as she went, the tiny splintering noises that a heart makes as it breaks. And she wondered if the sound was coming from her heart or from his.

PROSPECT

'Hello?' you say. 'Aubrey?'

'Hello Theney. What are you up to? It's been months. Must be three, four months.'

'Yeah, it has, I guess. I've been busy. I went to San Antonio. And I've been writing. I'm nearly finished a story I started a while back.'

'Writing? What's it about?'

'Hard to describe, really. I was wondering ... would you like to have a look at it?'

'Sure, if you want me to. Is it fiction? I don't usually read much fiction.'

'It's fiction. It's short. I'm having trouble with the ending.'

'Well, sure. I'd be ... happy ... to help. I've, ah, got someone here now. A student. We'll be done in thirty minutes. When did you want to come by?'

'Why don't I just drop it outside your door. Is the front door downstairs still propped open?'

He laughs. 'Yup.'

'Okay, I'll drop it by sometime late this afternoon.'

'Knock when you come by. I'd like to see you.'

'Maybe some other time.'

'You sure?'

'Just read the story.'

He pauses. 'Theney.'

'I'll see you,' you say, and hang up before he can say anything more.

You drive out to the west of town and stop by the side of the road, where the verge is covered in wild sunflowers. You pick twenty, thirty of them, and take them home and wash them down with water to freshen them and to remove the road dust. You pick some long grass and you mix it in with the sunflowers. You take the owl feather from the shelf where you've been keeping it and slip it into the bunch of flowers, then tie the bunch together with more grass. It looks like an offering to an ancient Greek goddess. Whatever.

When you place the bunch of flowers and the sheaf of paper outside his door, you feel a sense of lightness, and rightness, and you blow a kiss at his door for good luck, before heading down to Linklatters where you know Lloyd is working tonight.

TRISTESSA AND LUCIDO

Aubrey,
Can you help me with the ending?
Love Theney

PROSPECT

At Linklatters, Lloyd is busy and you sit on your stool and watch him work. He moves smoothly behind the bar, quiet and confident as he cycles through his work. He pours and mixes drinks, scrubs glasses before putting them in the little dishwasher behind the bar. He smiles, encourages, admonishes and sympathises. He somehow engages with all his customers. He learns instantly what a person is drinking and their preferences, and is there when they need him, away when they don't.

You watch Lloyd move and, remembering Rosa's words, you see the gift he brings. He looks across at you for a moment, and you raise your glass, without even thinking about it, saluting him.

He has not asked why you are here. You could not really have told him. And he probably already knows. You are here to wait. No more, no less. There is nothing you can do now, but wait. Be still and see what settles.

Driving downtown to Linklatters, the sun made it hard to see where you were going. As it moved towards the horizon, and sunset, you were blinded for a moment and had to squint at the road through partly closed eyes, using your lashes as a sunshade. The light was golden summer-evening light, the sort of light that makes you melancholy; makes you feel a sweet sadness for something lost but forgotten, an un-named lack, like a memory you used to have and all that remains is a memory of a memory.

In the late afternoon coolness of Linklatters, you hold your wine glass to your nose and breathe in the smell of Australian vineyards. Nostrils flaring, you search for something substantial, but it is simply wine.

'Lloyd,' you call him over.

'What's up, Theney?'

'Nothing. But I have to go to the bathroom. If Aubrey comes in, can you tell him I'll be back in a minute?'

'Sure thing, hon,' he says.

You make your way over to the stairs down to the basement. At the top of the stairs you stop for a moment and see how steep they are. You grab the handrail to make your way down, but after a couple of steps you let go and walk all the way down to the bottom, unaided. In the bathroom, you look in the mirror, and she smiles back at you.

When you go back upstairs, the sun has moved further down in the sky and beams of golden light are shining through the front windows. You see him. The light around him, silver and clear, makes you smile. You walk towards where he sits, on the stool beside yours. As you pass behind him, you touch him on the shoulder. He half turns and he is happy to see you. As you sit, he puts his hand on your neck, in that secret place beneath your hair.

Something clicks into place inside you. The smallest little sound, somewhere beneath your breastbone. Click.

ACKNOWLEDGMENTS

Thanks to all the people who were with me on this book's journey. I have relied on your support and inspiration in more ways than I can explain.

More specifically, I have to thank Monique Ridley who helped me finish the first draft by reading the weekly instalments I delivered to her when we worked together in North Sydney. Thanks to Wendy Hitchins for reading an early draft and being a wonderful friend. To Virginia Lloyd — thanks for listening between sets and putting me in touch with people who could help the manuscript become a book. To all at UQP who were 'just doing their job' — thanks. Madonna Duffy, 'my' publisher — thank you for your kindness and unstinting efforts. Many, many thanks to Belinda Lee, my editor. Thank you for making it feel easy, and for helping me produce a book that I know is a vast improvement on what you first saw. I am so grateful that UQP believes in and commits to the practice of editing a novel properly before launching it on an unsuspecting public. The editing process honours the writer, the reader and the publisher.